More Witchery
at Happy End

PAUL NEWNTON

PETER FRANCIS PUBLISHERS

Peter Francis Publishers
The Old School House
Little Fransham
Dereham
Norfolk NR19 2JP UK

First published 2010

A CIP Catalogue of this book is available from
the British Library

ISBN: 978-1-870167-45-1

This novel is entirely a work of fiction.
The names, characters and incidents portrayed in it are the work of
the author's imagination. Any resemblance to actual persons, living
or dead, events or localities is entirely coincidental.

Cover designed and typeset in Adobe Garamond 11½pt
by Chandler Book Design
www.chandlerbookdesign.co.uk

Printed in Great Britain by the
MPG Books Group, Bodmin and King's Lynn

Contents

Preface

Readers of the first book in the series *The Witch at Happy End* will know that Annabel, the wisewoman of Happy End does her best to help the village and its inhabitants live a happy life. In the first book, her efforts included thwarting the closure of the local school, an encounter with an artist masquerading under a false name and accused of murder, protecting the Pettit sisters' prize chrysanthemums and saving Jimmy Jepson's circus.

At the end of the book Annabel's daughter Betsy was stolen by fairies and our first story here begins with Annabel and Henry, her husband, lamenting the loss of their daughter.

A number of readers have been concerned about Betsy but I can assure them that Betsy does come home and is offered a place at the University of Brookshire. I have also been asked how the village got its name. Chapter 1 gives three versions of the story. You must choose the one you believe in.

Although this book follows on from the first it can be enjoyed on its own. Each story is complete in itself.

Paul Newnton
Gloucestershire

How the village got its name

Annabel looked at Henry and Henry looked at Annabel.
'I know, love; we don't seem to be complete without
Betsy. I wish she would come back to us.'

Long months had gone by since the fateful day when the
Fairy King had stolen Betsy away to hold her hostage for the
return of the golden amulet. The amulet had been returned
but he had decided to 'keep her for a while.'

Annabel still remembered returning home that night
desperately trying to think of ways to get Betsy back but
to no avail. She had to admit that fairy magic, especially
when wielded by the King of the fairies, was more powerful
than her own. So she and Henry sat lonely by their glowing
fire, Annabel knitting and Henry staring into space puffing
at his pipe.

Summer had turned to autumn, leaves were shedding

from the trees and the temperature was gradually dropping. One thing that Annabel had managed to do for Betsy was to put in her application to become a student at the University of Brookshire.

You will remember that Betsy had passed her exams and wanted to go to university in the coming year. Fortunately she had filled in the application forms just before she was spirited away. Annabel had checked that they were complete and had posted them off.

But let's leave Annabel and Henry and see what else is happening in the village that evening.

Life was going on much as usual. Richard Brown, who kept the Fox's Revenge, had a roaring fire in the inglenook fireplace by the bar and customers tended to gather round it as much as they could. One familiar figure who always got as close as he could to the fire was Foxy Sparrow. He was eighty one years old and spent a lot of his time in the pub apart from going to his sister's house for meals and wandering about on his own.

Richard didn't mind this, and since Foxy had a fund of stories he was always welcomed by the regulars. Mind you, they had heard most of the stories many times but for a free beer, Foxy would always tell them again, adding something new.

Foxy's favourite story was about how Happy End came to get its name. No-one actually knew how this had come about but many people had ideas, not the least of them Foxy.

This autumn night Foxy was sitting in his accustomed seat close to the fire when the door of the pub opened and a stranger blew in.

'Shut the door quickly,' Richard called. 'It's a cold windy night out there.'

All eyes turned towards the stranger who took off his raincoat, gave it a shake and hung it on the coat rack by the door. Then, turning to the assembled company he said, 'Good Evening,' and then to Richard, 'A pint of bitter if you please, landlord.'

Strangers in Happy End were always looked on with suspicion, but it turned out that this stranger was Ken Jenkins, a young reporter from the local paper The Barrow Magna Guardian. The newspaper was running a series on local names and their origins. The name Barrow Magna was an obvious one as the town lay on the other side of Barrow Hill. It was strange, he said, that there wasn't a Barrow Minor anywhere in the neighbourhood. He had heard that there might be one 'up North' but that was just hearsay.

In any event he had come, he said, to get a story about Happy End.

'Could anyone tell me,' he asked, 'how Happy End got its name?'

Richard looked around at the knowing faces of his customers and smiled.

'You had better ask old Foxy,' he said. He indicated the hunched up figure in front of the fire making his beer last as long as possible.

'He's our oldest inhabitant and what he doesn't know about it... well ask him yourself.'

Richard leant across the bar and spoke confidentially, 'A pint of beer might be a good idea to start him off.'

So carrying an extra pint, Ken Jenkins approached the old man who, despite his age, was still astute enough to know what was what. As the reporter approached, he drained his glass and set it down beside him. Almost before Ken had offered the pint, Foxy took it and said, 'Thank e young sir. You're a gent. Take a seat.'

A seat was found and the others in the pub gathered round the two figures in anticipation.

'Well young fella me lad,' said Foxy knowing pretty well what was coming next. 'And what can I do for you this bitter night?'

Ken was a bit taken aback by this direct approach but soon rallied and asked, 'What can you tell me about how the village got the name Happy End?'

'Ah now, that takes me back a bit,' said Foxy supping his beer with a reflective look in his eye. 'Let me see now.'

He looked slyly out of one eye at the young reporter.

'I don't suppose you've heard of Squire Tregellion?' he said.

'No,' said Ken, 'but you're going to tell me about him, aren't you? Do mind if I make some notes while you talk?'

He got out his reporter's notebook and a pen.

'Not a bit of it, not a bit of it,' said Foxy. 'As long as you keep me topped up.' He raised his glass and took a long pull at it.

'This was, of course, way back before my time, you realise, but this is how my father told it to me and how his father told it to him.'

Ken moved closer and opened his notebook.

'Old Squire Tregellion lived up at the Manor House where Colonel Blackley lives now but in those days it was called 'Happag's End'. It were all servants and footmen, coaches and horses, chamber maids and house maids, and a butler to rule over them. Lived in the grand style did the old Squire.'

Foxy drained his glass and held it out to Ken.

'How about another drink,' he said. Ken obediently took it to the bar to get a refill.

As he served him Richard asked, 'I don't know what Foxy is telling you but don't believe half of what he says.'

'Have you ever heard of Squire Tregellion?' asked Ken.

'Oh, he's telling you that one is he. Yes, Squire Tregellion, that's a good one.'

'You know the story,' said Ken eagerly.

'We all know it,' said Richard. 'At least what Foxy tells us, but I won't spoil the story. You go back over there and let him tell it his way.'

He handed Ken the beer, took his money, gave him change then, polishing the bar with a cloth said, 'Off you go, you're in for a treat tonight.'

Ken went back to Foxy and handed him his beer. After a long pull at it Foxy continued.

'So Squire Tregellion lived at Happag's End. Legend has it that the name dates back to Celtic times when there was an encampment on the spot where the Manor House is today. The leader of the tribe was a great chieftain called Happag the Red, on account of his red hair, you see. Well, after a fierce battle with a neighbouring tribe, Happag, mortally wounded, managed with the help of two of his faithful warriors to get back to his home. He died and ever after, the place was known as Happag's End. The house was named after the legend and the village, which was just one or two miserable damp cottages around the Manor at that time, also took the name Happag's End

'So, how did the name get changed?' Ken asked eagerly.

'Patience my young fella, patience. Rome wasn't built in a day and neither was Happy End. As I am sure you know, place names get changed over the ages, letters added and letters dropped and that's how it was with Happag's End. Happag became Happy and so there you have it.'

Ken had written this down in his notebook but didn't feel very satisfied with it.

'Is that it?' he asked.

'Well,' said Foxy, 'there is another explanation.' He waved his empty glass.

One pint later Foxy asked if he like poetry.

'I'm not too well up in it,' said Ken, 'Why do you ask?'

'There's some do say that the village is named after a poem. I'll recite it for you if you like.'

Foxy wiped the froth from his mouth and began,

'There is a place where witches dwell,
A village so I've heard it tell,
A place so far from strife and woe,
That friends and enemies safely go
To heal their wounds and blood feuds mend
The place's name is Happy End.'

He paused and looked at Ken out of the corner of his eye.
'You made that up,' said Ken.

'May be,' he said, 'but there have been witches in the village for generations. The most famous was old Mother Crawley. She was a witch, so they say. How she escaped being burnt or dunked in the pond, whatever they did in those days, I don't know. Of course, if she really was a witch then she probably used her powers to prevent it. Some said she had made a pact with the devil but my father said it was more likely that in her younger days she had made a pact with the Squire.'

That was obviously all Foxy was going to say so Ken thanked him and went over to the bar to ask Richard about it.

'You have heard two versions but if you want to hear another you should visit Henry Witchell, he's the unofficial Mayor of the village and he'll tell you another tale.'

'Should I phone him and ask if I can see him?' asked Ken.

'That's city ways,' said Richard. 'You just go along and knock on his door. If it's not convenient he'll soon tell you.'

So he did. Henry opened the door and after he had explained who he was and what he wanted, he was invited in.

'This is my wife Annabel,' said Henry and then to his wife, 'this is Ken Jenkins. He's come to hear the story of Happy End.'

Annabel shook his hand and said, 'Come and sit down by the fire. Can I get you a cup of tea or something?'

'No thank you,' said Ken settling into the armchair.

'So you want to hear how the village got its name,' said Henry sitting down on the settee by Annabel. 'It depends on which version you want to hear.'

'I've just heard Foxy Sparrow's versions over at the pub,' said Ken.

'You mean the warrior Happag?'

'Yes, that's right,' said Ken. 'Is there any truth in it?'

Annabel looked at her husband and laughed. 'Well there might be something in it, but tell him the story about King Arthur. That's the one I like best.'

Henry scratched his head. 'First you have to remember that there are many stories about King Arthur and the Knights of the Round Table and none of them may be true. The story I am about to tell you may also not be true but at least it is as true as Foxy's tale.'

Henry leant forward. 'There isn't much evidence that King Arthur actually existed, but if he did, then it's just possible that he was buried up on Barrow Hill. Other places lay claim to this but the story goes that he was mortally wounded in a battle with the Saxons near Bath about AD500 after the Romans had left our country and he was brought here quietly to die. Merlin was with him and legend has it that he lay in a dwelling place under Barrow Hill. His last words were, 'This is a happy place to end my days.'

'He died and was buried up on Barrow Hill. You can see the sacred grove of trees on the top of the hill to this day. Merlin and the knights left, but one of their knights remained behind so that he and generations to come would look after the King until he once more rose up to save the country from invasion.'

'So the village was known as Happy End,' said Ken.

'Yes,' said Henry. 'Somewhere in this village there is supposed to be a descendant of that knight who is here to guard the body and keep it from harm.'

'Surely that's just a story,' said Ken. 'Do you know who the guardian is?'

Henry hesitated and then said, 'The person you would least expect.'

'Who?' asked Ken.

Henry smiled. 'You won't believe this but it's rumoured that it's old Foxy Sparrow.'

'But, he has just told me these other stories,' said Ken.

'Foxy wouldn't tell you the truth if he was the guardian would he? He is known to go up the hill at least once a month and no-one knows where he goes,' said Henry.

'I know,' said Betsy stepping out of the shadows by the staircase.

'Betsy love, you fair gave me a fright,' said Annabel. 'Welcome back.' She went over to her daughter and gave her a hug.

'With her arm round Betsy she said, 'This is our daughter Betsy. She's been away for a while but now she's back.' She gave Betsy another hug. 'Ken is a reporter asking about the name of the village. What is it you know, love?'

'There is a king up there in the barrow under the hill,' Betsy said. 'He is lying in a glass coffin with a crown on his head and looks as if he is asleep. Foxy Sparrow visits him to make sure he is all right. I've seen him there.'

Henry looked quickly at his daughter and before Ken could ask any more questions he said, 'That's probably enough for tonight. Betsy is tired after her journey so I think we shall have to call it a night.'

'But, I've got so many questions for you,' said Ken. 'How do I know who to believe and what do I write up in the paper?'

'Go back to old Foxy and ask him. You've still got time before the Fox's Revenge closes. He is bound to be still there.'

'Why should he tell me that other story if he really is the guardian of King Arthur's tomb?' Ken asked.

'Why don't you ask him?' said Henry getting to his feet.

Annabel stepped forward. 'It was nice to meet you Mr Jenkins. I hope you find the answers you are looking for.'

Ken, rather bewildered, was led to the door and stepped out into the cold night air. As he went out he heard Annabel say to Betsy, 'Welcome home, love, tell us all about it.'

He made his way back to the pub and there as predicted was Foxy sitting in his usual corner by the fire.

'Back again,' said Foxy. 'What did you hear this time?'

Ken sat beside him. 'I heard that you are guardian of a king buried on Barrow Hill,' he said.

'That's a good story,' said Foxy. 'Worth at least another pint but I've had my fill for tonight.'

'But is it true?' asked Ken.

'There are folks who'd like to think so,' Foxy said. 'I bid you goodnight young sir.'

He put on his coat and raising his hat to the assembled company said, 'Goodnight to you all.'

The chorus of goodnights followed him to the door. He was a popular figure in the Fox's Revenge.

Ken was left standing by the fire as Foxy passed out of the door and vanished into the night.

2

Under the Hill

When the young reporter Ken Jenkins had left, Betsy sat down. Both Henry and Annabel were amazed at the change in her. She had left them as a young girl and had returned a mature woman. Not only that, she radiated an aura of confidence and power. However, in her eyes Annabel could see the young girl that she knew and loved.

'Can you tell us what happened?' she asked.

'Of course Mum,' Betsy was suddenly the young girl again anxious to tell of her adventures.

Annabel and Henry drew closer to the fire while the cat Ciaran lay curled up like a black furry ball on Betsy's lap.

'I almost don't know where to start,' she said. 'Such a lot happened after the Fairy King took me to the land of the fairies.'

'Just begin at the beginning and go on to the end,' said Annabel.

Betsy laughed, a liquid tinkling laugh that reminded Annabel of her own encounter with the Fairy Queen.

'Let me describe my first impressions then,' she said. 'We climbed to the top of Barrow Hill and went down into the hill. This was where I first saw the glass coffin containing the King. I don't know his name but the Fairy King said that he had been ruler of Britain many centuries ago, and, whenever the country was threatened his spirit would rise up to guard the British people.'

'But what happened in World War II.,' said Henry. 'I didn't see a ghostly king leading us to victory?'

'Hush, Henry. Let her tell it in her own way,' said Annabel.

Betsy continued, 'We went past the coffin and down into the hillside. At first it was just a dark passage lit by fairy lanterns but then we came to a large cavern where it was as light as day. It was as though we were walking through a village like our own, then we came to an orchard which contained trees of apple, pear, plums and damsons, figs, I think, and other fruits I didn't recognise. All of them had fruit hanging from their boughs and I was told later that the fruit is there all year round. We walked along a path between vegetable beds with beans and carrots, peas and potatoes, lettuce and tomatoes, sweet corn and strawberries, all varieties of vegetables and bushes of raspberries, loganberries, gooseberries and other fruits. Fairies were tending to them watering, hoeing and planting.

'There was a stream running down the right hand side of the garden and I could see fish leaping in the crystal clear waters. At length we came to a courtyard leading to the fairy castle with many buildings surrounding it. We passed through the courtyard and into the buildings, walking through to the Great Hall. The hall was decorated with gold and silver tapestries.'

Annabel nodded her agreement as she remembered her own visit to the Fairy Queen.

'The Fairy King led me into the Great Hall where the Queen sat on her throne attended by two fairies. The King sat on the second throne and held out his hand to the Queen.

'It's good to be back,' he said. 'We have recovered the amulet and I have brought Betsy Witchell to stay with us for a while.'

'Ah, yes, Annabel's child,' said the Queen. 'Welcome. As you are daughter of a witch we will instruct you in fairy magic so that when you go back to the world of mortals you will know and understand our ways.'

'And they did,' said Betsy. 'I was assigned a special teacher fairy. She grumbled a lot at first because the Queen had taken her away from instructing the young fairies in their duties but, as she became more used to me, she began to enjoy it.

'She told me that she had been a house fairy until the Queen had singled her out to be a teacher. I learnt that there are all sorts of fairies, each one appointed to do a particular job. There are ones for water, air, fire, and earth; fairies that look after the house, flowers, trees and the weather. Teacher fairies have to know something about all these and they instruct the younger fairies in their tasks.

'I can't tell you all the things I was taught, it would take to long, but I know about fairy medicine, fairy spells, how to call them when you need them, and how not to upset them as humans often do.

'I had a little house to myself with a house fairy in training to help me. She made the meals, washed up, cleaned the house, made the bed and did all the chores.

'I learnt about the King buried on top of the hill. They didn't know his human name but they called him Im-ne Bal which in their language means King-under-the-Hill. Two fairies guard him at all times and they have to report to Foxy Sparrow when he goes up there once a month.'

'I'm curious about this King,' said Henry. 'If he is King Arthur and it is true that he would look after Britain if it was ever threatened, why didn't he rise up and defend us in the Second World War?'

'You are thinking too much like a mortal,' said Betsy. 'His spirit did rise up in the war and he stiffened people's will to fight on and not be beaten, otherwise we might have been conquered. He is slumbering now but if ever there is a threat he will rise up again to stiffen the people's resolve.'

'But what's Foxy's part in all this?' asked Henry.

'I know that,' said Annabel. 'He goes up to make sure the fairies are guarding the King and then he sits by the side of the coffin and talks to him.'

'That's right,' said Betsy. 'He doesn't actually talk. I've seen him do it. He just sits there and thoughts flow back and forth between them. There is so much more to tell but I must go to bed. I feel as though I have been on a long journey.'

'Your room is just as you left it, love,' said Annabel. 'Fresh sheets and a clean nightdress. Sleep well, see you in the morning.'

*　　*　　*

Next morning Jack Jennings, the postman, brought a letter for Betsy. When she came down to breakfast she found it on her plate. Opening it, she exclaimed with pleasure. It was from the Department of Business Studies at the University of Brookshire inviting her for interview next week.

'You put my application in. Thanks Mum.' She got up and kissed Annabel on the cheek. 'I've got to be there next Wednesday at 2.30 pm.'

"How will you get there,' asked Henry who had finished his breakfast and was just about to go off to the Garden Centre.

Betsy thought for a moment.

'I'll catch the bus into Cirencester and get the Gloucester bus from there,' she said. 'I can't very well use magic can I.'

'I can take you in the truck if you like,' said Henry.

'That's nice of you Pa but won't that take you away from your work?'

'I've got a bit of business to do in Gloucester so it will fit in nicely,' he said.

'That's settled then,' said Annabel pouring the tea.

'I might come and take a look at the interview panel myself,' she said, with a twinkle in her eye.

'Don't you dare,' said Betsy. 'I want to do this on my own.'

Annabel didn't say anything; she just put the teapot back on its stand.

* * *

During the next few days Betsy slipped back into the familiar role of helping Henry with his plants and helping Annabel with her potions and the housework.

She began to talk more about her experiences under the hill as she watched Annabel make up a remedy for Mrs Cooke. From what she said about fairy medicine and some of the recipes she recited, Annabel realised that her daughter knew many things that she could only guess at.

Fairy magic and witch magic are two different things. In comparison with Annabel's magic, fairy magic is much more subtle and light of touch.

'I must write those recipes down,' she said. 'I recognise one or two of them from Old Mother Crawley's book She must have been in touch with the fairies herself.'

* * *

Soon it was Saturday and that afternoon there was a knock at the door. When Betsy answered it, it was Foxy Sparrow standing on the doorstep.

'Come in Foxy,' she said. 'I expect you want to see Mum.'

'No,' said Foxy, looking uncomfortable in what was probably his best suit although it showed signs of wear around the cuffs and lapels. 'No, it was you I've come to see.'

Foxy wiped his boots carefully on the mat and stepped into the house. Ciaran, the black cat, reared up and hissed at him as he passed.

'Don't worry about Ciaran,' she said. 'He's afraid of his own shadow. Come and sit down for a minute. What can I do for you?'

Foxy looked down at his feet.

'It's more what I can do for you,' he said. 'You know all about the King under the hill and I know you are looked on with favour by the fairies.'

'Yes, go on,' said Betsy.

Annabel came in at that moment. 'Oh, hallo Foxy. Is Betsy looking after you?'

'I was just about to ask Betsy if she would take on the job of guardian to the King,' he said. 'After I'm dead of course but at 81 years old I have to think of appointing a successor.'

Annabel smiled. 'You had better tell us a bit more about it first,' she said.

'To answer that I'd better go back a few years,' said Foxy. 'I think you both know the legend of the King buried under Barrow Hill.'

Annabel and Betsy nodded.

'That's not the whole truth of course but when I was a good deal younger than I am now I was walking on top of Barrow Hill among the trees when out of nowhere pops Arthur Jackson. He seemed fair worried that I had seen him and started questioning me about what I knew about this King. I didn't know anything about it and so, later on in the Fox's Revenge he told me about the legend. He told me that he was the guardian of the King, a position that had been handed down through his family for generations.

'He told me he had no son to hand on to and after a few pints I found myself agreeing to be the guardian when he died. He trained me in the task and it was fair scary at first but you get used to it. We used to go up and sit by the old King's coffin and I think if I stopped now I would miss it.'

'It's an interesting story,' said Annabel. 'But how can Betsy help you?'

Foxy looked nervously at Betsy.

'I've seen you up there with the fairies,' he said. 'Could you see it in your power to take my place when I'm gone? I've no son or daughter, you know and as far as I can see there's no reason why it must be always handed down through the male line. I've discussed this with the King and he agrees.'

'It was lovely of you to ask me,' said Betsy smiling, 'but I am afraid I must refuse. You see I shall be leaving the village soon to go to university so I wouldn't be much use to you.'

Foxy looked and sounded disappointed.

'If you don't do it then I don't know who to ask,' he said.

'I really can't Foxy, I'm sorry.'

'Perhaps I can help,' said Annabel.

'You mean you would do it?' said Foxy. 'I would never have dared to ask you, Mrs Witchell.'

'No,' said Annabel. 'I don't think I am the right person but I might be able to help in a different way.'

'How's that?' asked Foxy.

'Well,' she said. 'What you do seems very much like the job of church watcher. You know volunteers who sit in the Church for a few hours and talk to visitors if they need help. The Vicar has a rota of them for our Church.'

'You think one of them might do it,' said Foxy.

'Not necessarily, but often, the reason they do it is to pass the time when they are retired. They want to feel that they are doing something useful and keep in contact with people. Your 'King watching' seems to be a similar thing.'

'I hadn't thought of it that way,' said Foxy. 'But you are right; I would miss it if I stopped. What do you suggest?'

'I expect you have been pretty secretive about this up till now,' said Annabel.

'I have that,' said Foxy. 'That young reporter was ferreting around the other day so I told him a pretty tale about the name of our village.'

'Henry told him the other story,' said Annabel.

'I know,' said Foxy. 'Fair gave me a turn when he came back and asked me outright about it.'

'You ought to be proud to be the Guardian,' said Betsy.

'It's a noble tradition handed down from the Knights of the Round Table.'

'We don't know that for certain,' said Foxy but he drew himself up to his full height.

'I suppose it is a pretty noble thing,' he said. 'So what should we do?'

'Let it be known around the village. I'm sure they will all be proud of what you do and we may be able to find a volunteer.'

'I'm not too sure about letting it be known,' said Foxy. 'Let me go away and think about it. I'll get back to you in a day or so.' And off he went.

Over the next few days Annabel was so taken up with thinking about Betsy's interview that she forgot all about Foxy until she saw Griselda Griffiths in the village post office.

As Annabel came in, she heard Griselda discussing the King under the Hill.

'I believe old Foxy is going to appoint a successor soon,' she said.

Olive Garner, the post mistress, kept quiet as she had seen Annabel come in.

'I'm probably the one best qualified,' Griselda said unaware of Annabel's presence.

'Of course there's old Annabel over at Witchell's but she's a bit past it now.'

Annabel quietly tiptoed out of the shop, making sure that the shop bell didn't ring.

'Past it, am I,' she muttered between clenched teeth. 'I'll show her who is past it.'

Griselda Griffiths fancied herself as a witch and it was her meddling with a love potion that had landed Lucy Baxter and Lloyd Raven in a mess that had included Miss Tatt, the village school mistress, and Griselda's own husband.

Annabel went home muttering to herself and later that evening told Henry about it.

'Foxy must have decided to tell everyone as we suggested but there's one thing I'm certain of, Griselda Griffiths will never become the new Guardian.'

3

The Search for the Guardian

As Annabel discovered from Griselda Griffiths, Foxy
Sparrow had spread the tale around the village of his
search for a replacement Guardian to the King.

Actually, it wasn't very difficult. Someone once said that
you only had to sneeze at one end of the village and everyone
would know in a matter of minutes. It was usually the
Pettit sisters who spread the news but in this case Foxy had
mentioned it in the pub.

Lucy Baxter, the barmaid at the Fox's Revenge, had told
her mother and since she cleaned house for the Griffiths, it
had reached Griselda's ears quickly.

Knowing that Griselda wanted to become the Guardian,
made Annabel even more determined to select a suitable
replacement for Foxy. Someone much more suitable than
Griselda, who Annabel regarded as a meddling amateur

at least in the matter of witchery. But who could it be?

Annabel sat that morning in thought. She discounted the vicar, the Reverend Alistair Harding, and the doctor, Julian Everett. Who else could she ask? Certainly not the Pettit sisters. Names of everyone in the village ran through her mind. She knew she must act quickly otherwise Griselda Griffiths could use her powers on Foxy to convince him that she would be a worthy successor.

What made it more difficult was the need to think about Betsy getting ready for her interview at the University of Brookshire on Wednesday.

Betsy herself seemed quite unconcerned. She knew that her father would take her to Gloucester and bring her back so there was no problem there. As to the interview, she was a little nervous but her exam grades were good so she hoped it would just be a formality.

'I think you are worrying more than me,' she said to her mother on the day before the interview.

'Have you decided what to wear?' Annabel asked.

'Just a simple blouse and skirt,' said Betsy. 'I'll wear my long blue coat and knee length boots, that should keep me warm.'

'Don't worry about any work today, just relax and get ready.'

Betsy looked at her mother. 'I would rather do my normal work and get ready this afternoon. Let me help you this morning.'

'You could help. I'm puzzling about a successor to Foxy.

Help me think who we should ask to guard the King under the Hill.'

They sat down and made a list of everyone they could think of who might be suitable.

Annabel had already discounted the vicar, the doctor and the Pettit sisters. They added Miss Tatt and her assistant teacher Miss Wright to that list. Both Griffiths were discounted and they thought that Olive Garner at the Post Office Stores would be too busy although her husband Bill might be a possible.

'No point in considering the old folk,' said Annabel. 'That lets out Mr and Mrs Cooke and Mr Heathcote.'

'That's just a list of unsuitables,' said Betsy. 'So, who have we got left?'

'There's Tim Batsford, the blacksmith; two farmers, Ken Tuckett and Jack Brownley, but I expect they would be too busy.'

'Don't forget that it ought to be someone who is a believer,' said Betsy. 'You can't just ask anybody.'

'That narrows it down,' said Annabel. 'How about the young folk?'

'Certainly not Lucy Baxter,' said Betsy remembering Lucy's attempt to steal her friend Lloyd away from her.

'How about Lloyd?' asked Annabel.

'He is certainly a possibility,' said Betsy. 'I can ask him.'

'He's working in the greenhouses this morning. Henry wouldn't mind you talking to him.'

Betsy was just about to go into the Garden Centre to find

Lloyd when Eva Raven arrived, full of news. She had just come back from cleaning the Griffiths' house.

'Come in Eva. Have a cup of tea.'

'I don't mind if I do,' she said, putting her bag of cleaning materials down.

Annabel poured her tea.

'Did you know,' said Eva, 'Mrs Griffiths has been to see Foxy and offered herself as the Guardian thing. What do you think of that?'

'You had better wait, Betsy,' said Annabel. Then to Eva. 'I was afraid of that. What did Foxy say?'

'This is only what I overheard her telling her husband you realise.'

'Of course,' murmured Annabel. 'Go on.'

'Apparently she went to see Foxy telling him that she was a witch and that she was very suitable to be his successor.'

'What did he say?'

'He was a bit taken aback, or so she told her husband. He didn't say yes and he didn't say no. He just said he would think about it.'

'If he's got any sense he won't have anything to do with her,' said Annabel. 'I shall have to go and see him.'

At that time of day Annabel knew that she would find him in the pub so leaving Betsy to do the washing up she went over to the Fox's Revenge.

'Where's Foxy?' she asked Richard, the pub's landlord.

'Strange,' he said. 'He hasn't been in this morning. That's very unlike him.'

Annabel went back to her workshop and took out her crystal ball. Finding Foxy was easy. The crystal showed him making his way back down from Barrow Hill.

He's been up to see the King to discuss it with him, she thought. She had another look and to her surprise found him heading for her front door.

Betsy let him in and brought him out to the workshop.

Annabel greeted him and Betsy led him to a chair.

'I'll be off to see Lloyd now, Mum,' she said.

'No, wait,' said Annabel. 'Let's hear what Foxy has to say.'

'I'm fair bothered,' said Foxy twisting his cap in his hands. 'I went up to see the King to talk things over with him.'

Gradually Annabel got the story out of him. Griselda Griffiths had been to see him and had claimed the right to be the next Guardian.

'When she looked at me,' he said. 'I felt myself caught like a stoat in the beam of a flashlight. I couldn't move and when she told me she wanted the job I only just managed to delay agreeing. She must be a witch as I could feel her evil power over me.'

'Not so much of the evil power,' said Annabel. 'Not all witches are bad.'

'No disrespect, I'm sure,' said Foxy. 'Everyone knows you are a white witch, but that Griselda, she's a bad lot.'

'Do you want her to be your successor?' asked Betsy.

'I do not,' he said. 'I don't want anything to do with her putting the fluence on me like that.'

'I'll tell you what we'll do. Sit down Betsy and we'll all send out a message and see if we can find someone suitable for you.'

Foxy looked round the room at all the strange objects scattered around. He noticed Annabel's crystal ball, which was still in front of her.

'You mean by magic?' he said looking uneasy. 'Are you going to do all that eye of frog stuff?'

She smiled. 'No need for that. Just a simple message spell with the three of us concentrating, should do it.'

They sat round a small table in the corner with their hands touching and the crystal ball in the centre of the table.

'I want you both to close your eyes and concentrate on sending out a message to the Guardian to be, to come to us.'

'But, Mum, won't Griselda get the message and turn up here?' asked Betsy.

'That's a danger, of course, but hopefully we shall get a more positive result. Now concentrate.'

As they closed their eyes the shadows in the room seemed to lengthen, the room became dark in spite of the sunlight outside. Foxy gave a little shudder and closed his eyes. Betsy already had her eyes closed.

Annabel quietly intoned the words of a spell she had learnt from her mother and using the crystal to focus her thoughts, sent out a message to bring the person they wanted to them.

After what seemed an age Foxy opened his eyes and said, 'This is a waste of time. In any case, my mind keeps wandering.'

Without opening her eyes Annabel said, 'Stay with it, if you can, I can feel something happening.'

There was a timid knock on the workshop door. Annabel cautioned Foxy to be quiet, went to the door and opened it. To her surprise there stood Fred and Mabel Todd.

'Come in, come in,' she said.

It was unusual for so many people to come into her workshop but she had a few stacking chairs in the corner which Betsy dragged out for them to sit on.

'What can I do for you?' asked Annabel.

'We felt we had to come,' said Mabel. 'As you know we live up past the church and our children have grown up and left. Tony is at university in Hull and Sarah is married and gone to Australia.'

'We came to ask you about this Guardianship,' said Fred Todd. 'We didn't know Mr Sparrow would be here.'

'You want to be considered for the job,' said Foxy.

'Both of us really,' said Mabel. 'We have been church watchers for the past two years and we thought this sounded the same sort of thing.'

Annabel turned to them. 'Do you believe in fairies?' she asked.

'I do,' said Mabel. 'Aren't they supposed to live under the hill? I've never seen them but I have heard some strange tales. I don't know about Fred. We've never talked about it.'

'I'm a retired Chemistry Teacher,' said Fred. 'I try to examine everything scientifically so I don't believe or disbelieve. I'm open to evidence.'

Annabel looked at Foxy. 'There's your answer. What do you think?'

Foxy got up and walked around the pair.

'There's no reason why there shouldn't be two guardians. Yes, I think you will do. Report to me at the Fox's Revenge tomorrow morning at eight o'clock.'

Fred turned to Mabel. 'Could you make that ten o'clock?' he asked. 'Eight o'clock is a bit early.'

Foxy was just about to reply when there was a commotion outside the door and Griselda burst in looking hot and bothered.

'Too late,' said Annabel.

'What do you mean, too late?' said Griselda glaring at Foxy.

'The Guardians have been appointed,' said Foxy.

'You mean these two?' Griselda glared at Fred and Mabel who were trying to look as though they weren't there.'

'Yes,' said Annabel. 'And fine Guardians they will make. Go home Griselda and find someone else to bother.'

'You haven't heard the last of this,' Griselda hissed at the terrified pair.

With a look of hatred at Annabel she turned and swept out. Her impressive exit was a little marred by Ciaran running under her feet. She tripped and almost fell. She lifted her foot to kick the cat.

'Don't you dare,' Annabel's look spoke more than her words.

Griselda left rapidly.

After that, everyone felt a bit deflated but Fred and Mabel arranged to meet Foxy as planned at ten o'clock the next day.

When they had gone, Annabel's thoughts turned to Betsy's interview the next day.

'I will be all right, Mum, honestly you don't have to worry,' she said.

'I'm not worrying but I want to make sure you have the best chance of getting a place at university.'

'You promised no magic.'

'I haven't forgotten,' said Annabel. 'I might just take a look to see you are all right.'

And, there they left it until the next day.

4

All's Well That Ends Well

Wednesday dawned, the day of Betsy's interview.

Breakfast was a rushed affair as Betsy wanted to get ready and Henry was fussing. Annabel was glad when she finally waved them off.

Now, she thought, shall I leave this alone and let Betsy do it her way or shall I perhaps just have a peek at the situation to make sure everything goes well?

You can guess at the answer but before she went to her workshop she decided to finish her breakfast.

A nice piece of toast and another cup of tea. They won't get there for another hour at least, she said to herself.

Two cups of tea later she tickled Ciaran under his ears, fed him a saucer of milk, went into the workshop and set her crystal ball on the table.

She knew that Betsy's interview was at ten o'clock and

although it was only nine thirty she assumed that the interviewing panel would have assembled.

The original building for the University of Brookshire was very imposing set in its own parkland, but because of its rapid expansion many of the buildings dotted around the park were prefabricated or at least very temporary. The whole effect was that of an elegant Manor House set in a building site. The three interconnecting lakes which stretched down from the house were the nicest feature.

Annabel cast her crystal around the site, noticing the ducks and geese enjoying the water. Students were walking round the lakes on the circular footpath. She turned the crystal to the main car park and was able to locate Henry's truck. It was quite a walk up to the main house where the interviews were to be held and she was able to track them just walking up to the front door.

No sooner had she got them in her focus than Betsy turned round and looking straight at her in the crystal said, 'Mum, you promised.'

'I didn't actually promise,' said Annabel.

Betsy shrugged and turned away.

Following Betsy's progress Annabel saw Henry say goodbye and arrange to meet her in the car park after about ten thirty. Betsy was then shown into a room with five other candidates. As Annabel watched, the phone rang, breaking her concentration.

I should never have a phone in my workroom, Annabel thought. She lifted the receiver.

It was Mabel Todd speaking in a very scared voice.

'We need your help Annabel. We can't get out of the house and we are supposed to meet Mr Sparrow at ten o'clock.'

'What do you mean, can't get out of the house?' asked Annabel.

'All of the house doors seem jammed and Fred has tried getting out of a window and that is jammed to. Can you get someone to let us out?'

'Hang on,' said Annabel. 'I think I know what has happened. I'll deal with it as quickly as I can. In the meantime, don't panic; just sit tight until you hear from me.'

'Thanks Annabel,' Mabel sounded relieved. 'Be as quick as you can.'

I'm sure it's that dratted Griselda casting a spell to stop them meeting Foxy, she thought. This would happen just when I want to watch over Betsy.

Annabel decided that the best way to deal with it was to go out-of-the-body as she could get to the Todd's house quickly and then be able to undo the spell. Putting the crystal away, she went up to her bedroom and was soon hovering above her body.

In a flash, she was at the front door of the Todd's house. As she tried to slip in through the door, an invisible force held her back.

'Right, Griselda Griffiths. You asked for this.' She circled the house three times incanting a spell as she went.

Griselda's spell broke and this time Annabel went

straight into the sitting room where Fred and Mabel were sitting on the settee, looking dejected. The next problem was how to communicate with them, as she couldn't be seen in her out-of-the-body state. Fortunately she had experienced this problem before and was able to make the telephone ring.

When Mabel picked up the phone at first it sounded as though there was no-one there, then Annabel spoke.

'Mabel, it's me, Annabel. Try opening your door now, it should be all right.'

'Annabel, where are you, it sounds as if you are speaking inside a tin can?'

'Never mind that,' Annabel said. 'Just get down to see Foxy and watch out for Griselda Griffiths.'

Annabel was certain that Griselda had trapped them in their house so that she could go and meet Foxy and persuade him to use her as the Guardian.

No time to worry about that now, she thought. I might as well get over to the University and see how Betsy is getting on.

In her out-of-the-body state she was quickly able to transport to the room where Betsy was talking to one of the other candidates, a girl called Jessica.

It was obvious that Jessica was really worried about the interview and Annabel was pleased to see that Betsy was using a calming spell to relax her. Betsy herself didn't seem at all worried so Annabel decided to take a look at the interviewing committee.

Floating into the oak panelled room where four people sat round a table Annabel 'sat' for a moment in the interview chair and took a look at them.

They were discussing how they would handle the questions. Annabel took an instant dislike to the one they called Ted, on the far left, as all he seemed to do was object to everything that was said. The chairman, whose name turned out to be Professor Lawrence, was Head of the Business Studies Department and he seemed very tolerant. Certainly, he listened patiently to everything Ted was saying. The other two members of the panel were women, one had red-hair and a green dress that set off her colouring well and was obviously a very prominent member of staff, the other was a dowdy female who said very little.

Annabel got out of the chair hurriedly as the first candidate was shown in. She moved over to the wall. She still found it strange to be able to observe without anyone seeing her.

The candidate was a boy about Betsy's age who put up a good showing in spite of Ted trying to put him down.

Annabel got a bit bored by the proceedings as it was obvious that, unless there was something major, all candidates were going to be given places.

When Jessica came in, Annabel could see that Betsy had done a good job in relaxing her, but the lecturer called Ted was absolutely horrible to her and she left the room crying.

Next in was Betsy who walked confidently up to the interview chair and sat down.

I'm not having this, thought Annabel and put a spell on Ted before he could begin to speak. He doubled up in agony and managed to croak, 'I'm sorry Professor Lawrence, you must excuse me.' He left the room rapidly, heading for the toilet.

'Shall we continue?' Professor Lawrence asked and the others, looking relieved, nodded their agreement.

After that, it was plain sailing for Betsy and she left the room elated. Annabel went back into the other room where Betsy was consoling Jessica and telling her about the awful lecturer and how he had to leave. She shot a knowing glance over to the corner of the room where Annabel stood.

She can see me, thought Annabel.

Yes, I can, Mum, Betsy thought back. Thank you for dealing with that obnoxious person. See you back at home soon.

Annabel waved and headed for the Fox's Revenge where she knew the next drama would be developing. Sure enough, there was Foxy outside the pub with Griselda. She obviously had him in some sort of trance.

Just as Annabel arrived, Mabel and Fred came down the road. Griselda turned, looked surprised and began to move Foxy away towards Barrow Hill.

Annabel allowed Griselda to lead him up the hill, throwing out a thought to Fred and Mabel for them to follow.

Foxy stumbled up the path looking dazed closely followed by Griselda. She turned on Fred and Mabel and said in an unpleasant voice, 'Stay away. You're not wanted here.'

A true witch would have used a spell to stop them but Annabel guessed that as an amateur she got her spells out of books. Without a book in front of her, she was relatively helpless.

Still, reflected Annabel. Even a wounded animal can be dangerous.

They arrived at the top of the hill.

Griselda looked around and then commanded Foxy to take her into the barrow.

Foxy went towards the entrance but before Annabel could use a spell to stop them, the terrifying figure of the Fairy King appeared in front of the entrance.

Griselda dropped to her knees. There was a flash and she disappeared.

The Fairy King turned to Foxy who, released from the trance that he had been under, recoiled from his dominating presence.

'No need to be afraid,' he boomed. 'I have sent her back to her home with her memory wiped clean of this incident. She will never bother you again.'

He turned to Fred and Mabel. 'Welcome and enter,' he said. 'You will make fine guardians of the other King who is buried here.'

Foxy led them into the hill.

When they had gone the King turned to Annabel.

'You now have your daughter back and Mr Sparrow has his successors,' he said. 'So all's well that ends well.' He disappeared.

Annabel returned to her body just in time to greet Betsy returning with her father from Gloucester.

The School Play

Rabbits, fairies and jolly jack tars all mixed up together. It was rehearsal time for the school play.

Once a year Miss Tatt and Miss Wright had to think up an entertainment where as many children as possible dressed up and appeared on stage before their doting parents.

This time the theme was a little confused but the play was to begin with a chorus of sailors singing 'Over the ocean blue' while a cardboard ship jerked its way across the backcloth heading for a tropical island which was the subject of the next scene. Two children holding hands wandered in front of the sailors heading for the island. The island was obviously a fairy island as children in a variety of gauzy wings hurtled about chasing hopping bunny rabbit children in total confusion.

Miss Tatt held up her hands in horror. 'Children, children, Stop!'

Most of the children took it literally, bunny rabbits stopped with their arms and legs in unnatural postures, fairies poised with wands outstretched.

Miss Tatt turned to Miss Wright. 'Can you sort them out? I want to have a word with Annabel.'

Annabel was sitting at the back of the school hall, watching the proceedings with amusement. She had been called in to help, as in the next scene the wicked witch came to cast a spell on the two children to stop them from getting home. The fairies would outwit the witch and send the children safely home with the chorus of sailors singing 'I do like to be beside the seaside' although what that had to do with the children getting home safely was beyond Miss Tatt's comprehension. Miss Wright had suggested it as 'something for a rousing finish.'

Annabel wasn't sure about being called in as an expert on wicked witches but had done her best to supply Angela Wilkins, the girl who was to play the witch, with a pointed hat, a black cloak and broomstick. Henry had made the broomstick out of a branch and twigs from a tree in the garden. She pointed out to Miss Tatt that the girl should also have a hooked nose ('I'm not sure if we are expert enough to do that' Miss Tatt said) and a humped back.

All the costumes had been made by the mothers from odds and ends, resulting in colourful but bizarre effects.

Miss Wright had sorted out the rabbits and the fairies and was now beginning the scene where the two children were asleep on a rock, when in comes the wicked witch.

'Come on Angela,' Miss Wright called. 'Time for the wicked witch.'

Annabel whispered, 'Go on Angela, you can do it.'

Bending double and waving her broomstick, Angela, who was actually a very pretty child, gave a creditable imitation of an old crone, croaking out a made up spell to keep the children asleep forever.

Miss Tatt had asked Annabel about the wording of the spell. 'Not because we want a real one of course, but it has to sound right.'

Annabel considered this. 'How about: Hokus, pokus, sleep my pretties, stay right here until you drop, I will rock you through the ages, never back home to pop.'

Miss Tatt laughed. 'I would say that will do very well.'

Angela was croaking out the spell over the children while the fairies and bunnies watched from behind a collection of papier mâché rocks.

'Now,' said Miss Wright. 'Come on fairies, surround the witch and zap her with your magic.'

They hadn't been quite sure how to handle this but Annabel said it would be all right if they surrounded the witch, holding hands and dancing round her singing 'Witch, Witch go away, don't come back for many a day. Break the spell, release the bonds, do it as we wave our wands.' Then they should cluster round Angela who gets a chance to slip out of sight.

It didn't go too well in the rehearsal as in order to surround the witch they had to dance round the two sleeping children and some rocks were in the way.

Miss Tatt clapped her hands. 'Let's try that again. Witch and fairies a bit farther forward this time.'

The rehearsal went on until at the end the troupe of jolly jack tars came on, joined by the rest of the cast, including the witch, to sing 'Oh we do like to be beside the seaside.'

Miss Tatt collapsed into a chair.

'I think this will be the best one yet,' she said mopping her brow. 'I just hope it will be all right on the night.'

'I am sure it will,' said Annabel and then as Angela jumped off the stage, 'Nice Angela. Try to make it a bit more menacing when you say the spell but otherwise very good.'

'Thanks Mrs Witchell,' Angela said in a very unwitchlike voice.

*　*　*

Excitement in the village ran high. Children love dressing up and everyone except Jason Wilkins were happily getting ready for the big day.

Jason was used to being in the limelight, he had won a prize at the village fete and was always asking questions in class. Miss Tatt regarded him as a bit of a menace as he always pushed himself forward. In last year's play based on the Nativity, he had played the part of one of the wise men and had practically wrecked the performance by over-acting. That was why she hadn't given him a part in this year's play.

'I feel terrible about leaving Jason out as he is always so willing but we can't risk last year's fiasco,' she confided in Miss Wright.

Meanwhile Jason was complaining to his gang.

'I'm just too good for them,' he said to Tim, Charley and Robin.

Tim Brownley was the young son of Jack Brownley the farmer to the north of the village, Charley Everett was the doctor's son, and Robin was the offspring of an inoffensive couple called the Darlings. Together with Jason as their leader, they constituted the 'Barrow Hill Boys' at least that's what they called themselves. Their meeting place was the old scout hut, which, largely abandoned, lay beside the new village hall to which all the village happenings had now been transferred.

The Barrow Hill Boys favourite reading was the Just William books and they tried to imitate the adventures in the books whenever they could. Angela, Jason's sister, was always trying to join the gang but they wouldn't let her.

'We don't want a girl in the gang. Girls are too much trouble,' Tim was very definite about this. Charley wasn't so sure as he had an older sister Charlotte and didn't find her any trouble, Robin did not express an opinion.

Jason had called the gang together to discuss an idea.

'Why should my sister be in the play when I haven't got a part?'

'Because she is better than you,' said Charley.

'No she isn't,' said Jason. 'I've got a plan, listen.'

Jason's plan consisted of getting Angela to run an errand for her mother, making her think that she had plenty of time. He would trick her by putting the time on the clock in the hall back one hour. So, Angela would set off on her errand thinking she had time before the performance, arriving back too late to stop Jason changing places with her as the witch.

'It sounds simple,' said Tim. 'I'll bet something goes wrong.'

'Nothing can go wrong,' said Jason. 'I've thought it out in great detail. Just leave it to me.'

* * *

The great day dawned and gradually the excitement mounted. It was to be an evening performance so Miss Tatt let the children out early from school so that they could get ready.

Angela went up to her bedroom and started to get into her costume when Jason told her that their mother wanted her to run an errand.

'Why can't you do it?' Angela said angrily. 'You're not in the play.'

'I don't know why she wants you to do it,' said Jason. 'You have plenty of time.'

He had already put the hall clock back one hour.

Angela went downstairs but her mother was nowhere to be seen. Jason followed his sister down and pointed to a small package on the hall table.

'I know she wanted you to take this parcel to Mrs Cooke.'

Angela stamped her foot. 'Blow and bother,' she said but after looking at the clock and satisfying herself that there was time, she put her coat on and left the house.

Jason went back upstairs and was soon attired in the witch's costume.

*　*　*

Back at the school, the Jolly Jack Tars: Tim, Charley and Robin were busily applying moustaches and beards to each other with burnt cork. Jason arrived and was skulking in a corner trying not to be seen. Miss Tatt and Miss Wright were too busy to notice him as they had fairies panicking, that that their wings were on straight, that their costume was too small, their headdresses were on crooked.

Annabel, on the other hand, wanting to make sure that Angela was happy in her part, came across Jason hiding in a corner.

'Hallo, Jason,' she said. 'What's all this about?'

'Angela couldn't come,' he said. 'So I took her place.'

At that moment Miss Tatt called, 'Curtain up in five minutes.'

Annabel stood and looked at him for a moment.

'I think you and I had better make some magic,' she said. 'Hold my hand, we haven't got much time.'

In an instant, they were at Mrs Cooke's door where a bewildered Angela was trying to explain why her mother had sent her with an empty parcel.

Angela rushed up to Annabel. 'What's happened? Why are you here Jason?'

Annabel let go of Jason's hand and patted Angela reassuringly.

'Jason, take off the outfit and Angela you put it on. Don't worry Mrs Cooke, just a misunderstanding. We've just got time to get back.'

Jason was quite clumsy in taking the witches outfit off but eventually Angela was able to put it on.

'Hold my hand,' said Annabel. 'No, not you, Jason. You stay here.'

Jason was left clad in vest and underpants while Annabel and Angela were instantly transported back to the school hall.

'There you are Angela,' said Miss Tatt. 'I was looking for you everywhere.'

'Sorry Miss Tatt,' Angela said, looking at Annabel with wonder.

She whispered, 'Is that what witches do?'

Annabel looked thoughtfully at her. 'Sometimes,' she said. 'Mainly when we are in a hurry otherwise we can use other methods.'

'I want to be a witch when I grow up,' she said.

'Maybe,' said Annabel. 'Hurry now, the curtain is going up.'

*　*　*

The play was a great success.

'Angela wants to be a witch when she grows up,' Annabel told Henry and Betsy afterwards.

'I thought you had to be born to it like me,' said Betsy.

'Not necessarily,' Annabel replied. 'You have to be pretty serious about it though and get a witch to take you on as an apprentice. In Angela's case, the play put the idea into her head. I don't think she was really serious.'

'What about Jason?' asked Henry.

'Mrs Cooke was very kind to him,' she said. 'She gave him a piece of cake and a drink and sent him off home in one of Mr Cooke's old raincoats. I heard that he got a good talking too afterwards for altering the clock.'

6

Catch me if you can

Mr Tomkins suddenly presented himself at the Fox's Revenge and wanted to stay for the week. Richard Brown, proprietor of the pub, had just made the three bedrooms en-suite and was anxious to promote the pub as a bed and breakfast opportunity for tourists. The main problem as he saw it was the lack of things for them to do in a sleepy little village like Happy End. However, the arrival of Mr Tomkins changed all that.

Mr Eric Tomkins was a short weedy man who looked out on the world through pebble lens glasses. He asked if Richard would be prepared to offer a packed lunch and an evening meal as well as bed and breakfast.

Since Mr Tomkins had arrived by the morning bus and there was nowhere else to eat in Happy End Richard felt that in the tradition of all innkeepers he ought to agree. He discussed it with his wife Gladys and so they offered Mr T full board.

He explained his reason for wanting a packed lunch. His hobby was bird watching and he wanted to explore the village and Barrow Hill to see what birds there were in the area.

Richard was enthusiastic about offering food in the pub. 'It might bring more tourists into the area and some of the locals might want a bite to eat.'

Gladys wasn't quite as enthusiastic.

'Do we want more tourists in the area?' she asked. Privately she was thinking of the extra work that the cooking would place on her.

'We might have to bring someone else in to help me with the food if this takes off,' she said.

'Early days yet,' said Richard. 'But we will keep it in mind.' He gave his wife a hug.

After paying for the week in advance, Mr Tomkins was given the best of the three bedrooms and on the first morning, a Saturday, set off to explore the village. It was at this point that he came to the attention of the Barrow Hill Boys.

After the school play, Jason's credibility with the Barrow Hill Boys had suffered a little. He felt that Tim, slightly taller than he was, always wanted to be leader of the gang. In order to maintain his position he had to think of something new. The ideal situation presented itself in the form of Mr Tomkins.

The gang enjoyed tracking people as Jack Jennings, the postman, knew to his cost. They thought that he couldn't see them but their tracking methods consisted of hiding behind a wall and popping out when they thought he wasn't looking. He had tired of them following him around the village. A sharp word to Jason's father had stopped it but tracking people was one of the gang's specialities so Mr Tomkins was a godsend.

Mr Tomkins was so short sighted that it is doubtful if he would have noticed them standing right in front of him. At first he explored the village even to the extent of wandering up people's paths and looking round their gardens. He seemed to find nothing wrong in this and if challenged would smile vaguely and lift his hat in acknowledgement.

'What is he doing?' asked Robin.

'I think he's a spy,' said Tim. 'He's spying out the land, looking for a place to hide secret documents.'

In the afternoon, Mr Tomkins set off up Barrow Hill with a pair of binoculars round his neck. The gang had nothing to do, so they followed him. They couldn't apply their usual tracking techniques to Barrow Hill but they adapted to hiding behind hawthorn bushes and the copse of trees at the top.

His behaviour was peculiar. When he got to the top of the hill, he reached into the bag he was carrying and pulled out a collapsible butterfly net.

'I thought he was a bird watcher?' whispered Charley. 'How is he going to catch birds in a butterfly net?'

'What does he want to catch them for anyway?' asked Jason.

The gang had no answers but continued to watch. They tracked him across the top of the hill and down the other side towards the town of Barrow Magna. He seemed to be looking for something but what it was they couldn't establish. In the end, they gave up and went home for their tea.

*   *   *

Meanwhile, Rosemary and Emily Pettit were calling on Henry and Annabel.

'It's terrible,' twittered Emily accepting a cup of tea from Annabel.

'They were gold earrings handed down to us by our mother and now they have gone,' said Rosemary.

'Perhaps you have just misplaced them,' said Henry.

'No, they are always in the glass dish on the dressing table in my room,' said Emily.

'That's not all,' Rosemary broke in. 'We have heard of two other thefts in the village in the last day or so.'

The Pettit sisters were the eyes and ears of the village. Nothing escaped them.

'What sort of thefts?' asked Annabel.

'Silly things really,' said Rosemary. 'The key to Mrs Cooke's outside toilet and Mollie Pike's wedding ring.'

'There's no sense in that,' said Annabel. 'Let us know if you hear of anything else and I'll try to help.'

She discussed it with Henry after they had gone.

'There's usually a pattern to thefts,' Henry said. 'But this makes no sense. I thought the Pettit sisters were going to accuse Eva Raven as she goes in to clean for them once a week.'

'Eva's as honest as the day is long,' said Annabel. 'Anyway she doesn't clean for Mrs Cooke. Mollie is back with John Pike so she looks after him and the house, so it can't be Eva.'

'What about strangers in the village?' asked Henry.

'There's only that Mr Tomkins staying over at the Fox's Revenge and by all account he's harmless enough.'

Although Annabel had said he was harmless, the thought stayed in her mind. She reasoned that the thefts had to be due to someone outside the village and Mr Tomkins was the only stranger. Also, how could you account for the strange nature of the thefts, earrings, a key and wedding ring?

Annabel shrugged her shoulders and got on with mixing up a cure for Mrs Twitchett's rheumatics.

That evening she had another idea.

'You don't think Jason Wickens and his gang had anything to do with it?' she said to Henry.

'Well, it is the sort of thing that boys might get up to for devilment,' Henry lit his pipe thoughtfully. 'They are always trailing around the village. It might be some sort of game?'

'I'll have a word with them,' said Annabel and next day she tracked them down to the scout hut where they were holding their morning meeting.

They were seated on old boxes round a packing case, munching biscuits and drinking lemonade. They got up as she came in but she motioned them to sit down.

'I need your help,' she said.

The gang had wondered what they had been doing wrong but at this they visibly relaxed.

'Always ready to help,' said Jason. 'Just say the word.'

Tim pulled up another box and after carefully examining it for nails Annabel sat down.

'It's like this,' she said. 'You and your gang see everything that's going on in the village so I would like to ask a little favour.'

They drew closer and Tim offered her a biscuit.

'No, thank you, Tim. Mind you this is confidential, just between you and me.'

They all nodded agreement.

'I expect you have heard that there have been some thefts in the village and we have to find out who is doing them.'

Charley spoke up, 'My father was over at the Pike's place treating Mr Pike for a cut arm and he told me about Mollie Pike's wedding ring.'

'What do you want us to do?' asked Jason.

'Just keep your ears and eyes open and report anything you find out back to me,' said Annabel.

After she had left, the gang went into a huddle.

'I'll bet you it's that Mr Tomkins,' said Tim. 'Perhaps he's stealing things, hiding them on the hill, then when he's got enough loot he will go to a fence and get money for them.'

The Barrow Hill Boys ideas on thieves and thieving were based on what they read and saw on television.

*   *   *

'They don't have anything to do with this,' Annabel told Henry later. 'If they had I would have known. Now I've given them the task of finding the thief.'

The Barrow Hill Boys loved this. A real task and one which involved poking their noses into everything and shadowing everyone.

'I say we make Mr Tomkins prime suspect,' said Jason. 'All those in favour.'

'I vote we each take a person and follow them,' said Tim.

'That's no good,' said Jason. 'Far better to stick together and work as a team.'

In the end, it was agreed that they would shadow Mr Tomkins. However this was going to be difficult as the next day was Monday and they could only shadow him after school had ended.

Jason told Annabel of their decision but said plaintively, 'Of course he can get up to all sorts of things while we are in school.'

'Don't worry about that,' said Annabel. 'I can arrange to take care of him during the day.'

Birds make good watchers and Annabel called on one of the many pigeons that inhabited the trees near the Garden Centre. This particular one was a favourite of hers and it answered to the name of Fred. It was quite tame and came into her workshop where it stood on the workbench pecking the seed that she had put there.

Annabel explained what she wanted and Fred fixing her with a beady eye bobbed his head and after a final peck at the seed set off on its errand.

Fred's mission was to follow Mr Tomkins and report any unusual behaviour. As pigeons don't have much to do except eat, make love to other pigeons, ponder the mysteries and meaning of life, and sleep, Fred was quite pleased to carry out this task.

It located Mr Tomkins going up the path to Barrow Hill and circling high above followed his progress. Mr T took out his butterfly net and was searching among some low hawthorn bushes when Fred became aware that he wasn't the only one watching. A magpie was sitting on a nearby tree branch and as the man moved so did the bird. Fred's first thought was that Annabel had asked both of them to act as watchers but then Fred reasoned she would have told him.

The day wore on and both birds stayed watching. Fred knew that the magpie would be aware of him but it made no attempt to make contact. In the end, Mr T gave up searching the hillside and went back to the Fox's Revenge. Fred reported to Annabel.

*　*　*

Mr T was neither a thief nor a birdwatcher. He was in fact author of a book called 'The Fairies at the Bottom of Your Garden.' He had heard that fairies inhabited Barrow Hill and had come there to catch one, hence the butterfly net. Since he had never seen a fairy and had based his notions largely on Sir Arthur Conan Doyle's book 'The Coming of the Fairies' he thought fairies were little creatures, whereas we know from Annabel's encounters with them that they are more the size of small children.

*   *   *

After Fred the pigeon had reported back to Annabel she realised that she would have to take more of a hand in the investigation. So next day she was in her workshop, about to take out her crystal ball when the Fairy Queen materialised in front of her.

Annabel was quite surprised as she had never seen the Fairy Queen away from Barrow Hill.

The Fairy Queen read her thoughts and said, 'This is an emergency. We need your help.'

'Of course, anything I can do,' said Annabel. 'What's the problem.'

'Mr Tomkins is the problem. He is searching the hill trying to catch a fairy. All my people are afraid to go out while he is about. Can you help us?'

'Why can't you simply use your magic to confuse him,' said Annabel.

'We have been doing that but we need a more permanent solution. That's why I have come to you.'

They talked together for a while and decided on a plan.

Next day Mr Tomkins went up the hill as usual with his butterfly net.

'If I don't catch anything today I shall give up,' he muttered to himself.

Then, to his surprise and delight among the trees at the top of the hill he saw what looked like a butterfly. On coming closer, he could see that it was a tiny person with highly coloured wings sprouting from its back.

As he brought his butterfly net closer, it saw him and fluttered away. He followed.

If you have ever tried to catch a butterfly you will know that it often manages to stay just out of reach. So it was for Mr T. Just as he was about to bring the net down, off it went again. What he didn't realise was that it was luring him on farther and farther towards one of the entrances to the hill.

He saw what looked like the entrance to a cave in front of him. The 'fairy' fluttered inside and he followed. The entrance closed behind him and he was trapped.

Of course it wasn't a real fairy it was just a projection designed just to get him into the hill.

He looked around. He was in a small cave with passages leading from it. The cave was lit by small twinkling lanterns.

'Don't be afraid,' a voice said. He turned and there he saw what looked like a small child but when he looked more closely, peering through his pebble lenses, he saw wings folded behind her back. The tiny fairy projection had vanished.

Recovering slightly, he asked, 'Are you a fairy?'

'Some call us 'the little folk,' she replied. 'Come, I'll take you to our Queen.'

Mr T had to bend almost double to get down the passageway but then they came to a large cavern where it was as light as day. They walked through what appeared to be a small village and then came to an orchard, walking along the path between vegetable beds. Mr Tomkins was amazed at the variety of vegetables and fruit. He was surprised to see so many, what he took to be, small children. Following his guide, he went into the castle where the Queen sat on her throne attended by two fairies. There were so many things to take in that his mind was reeling.

The Queen rose to greet him and led him over to an alcove at the side.

'I expect you wonder why you are here?' she said.

Mr Tomkins thought that he had never before heard such a wonderful melodious voice.

The Queen went on. 'I believe you are the author of a book about us?'

Mr T found his voice, 'Yes, your majesty,' he stammered.

'Unfortunately you based your book on the Cottingley Fairies which, as you must know, were cardboard cut-outs photographed by Elsie Wright and Frances Griffin in 1917.'

'I know there is some doubt about the authenticity of the photographs,' he said, 'but how can you explain the fairy I saw on the hillside. It looked just like the photographs.'

The Fairy Queen smiled. 'That was just designed to bring you here so that I could talk to you. You must have seen the real fairies all about you as you came through the gardens?'

'Yes, I did, but I thought they were small children pretending to be fairies.'

'You have a lot to learn,' said the Queen. 'I am going to put you with one of our teaching fairies who will instruct you in our ways. The book you eventually write about us will then be much more accurate.'

Mr Tomkins' mind was still full of wonders as the teaching fairy led him away.

Meanwhile back at the village Jason and his gang had been looking for Mr Tomkins but reported to Annabel that he seemed to have disappeared. Richard Brown at the pub was worried as it seemed that Mr T had left without paying his bill.

Annabel of course knew what had happened and expected Mr Tomkins to reappear in a few days time, a much wiser and happier man.

With nothing better to do, Jason's gang continued searching for him climbing trees on top of the hill. There they discovered a magpie's nest full of shiny paper, brass screws and other oddments and in the middle of the nest they found the Pettit's golden earrings, the key to

Mrs Cooke's outside toilet and Mrs Pike's wedding ring. They bore them triumphantly to Annabel who told them that magpies often steal bright objects and asked if they knew the old rhyme. They said they didn't, so she recited it to them.

One magpie for sorrow, Two for joy, Three for a girl, Four for a boy, Five for silver, Six for gold, Seven for a tale never to be told, Eight for a wish, Nine for a kiss.

'What does a tale never to be told mean?' asked Robin.

"I don't know," admitted Annabel. "The rhyme has many versions. This is the one my mother taught me.'

She asked them to take the things back to their original owners with an explanation. This they did and were rewarded with tea and cake at Mollie Pike's, a 'thank you' from Mrs Cooke, and wonder of wonders, a fifty pence piece from the Pettit sisters.

Two days later, Fred the pigeon arrived at Annabel's workshop to tell her that Mr Tomkins was making his way down the hill. She walked over to the Fox's Revenge just in time to meet him.

'How did you get on?' she asked.

Mr Tomkins was a changed man. He was striding along and Annabel noticed that he wasn't wearing his pebble lens glasses.

'I met the fairies,' he said. 'They weren't anything like I imagined. I've got so much detail from them I'm almost bursting. They told me I must never tell where I got my information. I must never tell about Barrow Hill and what lies beneath. In return, they gave me the gift of sight. See I don't need these anymore.'

He waved his spectacles at her. 'This is going to be the best book on fairies ever.'

7

Scarecrows

Spring had sprung in Happy End. Plants were putting forth fresh green shoots, daffodils were in full bloom, the world was alive with birdcalls, insects were buzzing and the trees were mantled in pale green leaves.

Jack Brownley was talking to Richard Brown in the Fox's Revenge.

'You don't realise what a heavy burden of responsibility the seasons place on the farmer,' he said.

Jack kept the farm just up past the church, cultivating the fields around Happy End.

Richard, owner of the Fox's Revenge, leant over the bar.

'What sort of responsibility?' he asked.

'For one thing, we need to look after the young seeds as they germinate. Did you know that one crow can dig up a whole row of germinating corn in less than an hour?'

'Don't you use scarecrows to keep them off the fields?' Richard asked.

Jack laughed. 'Scarecrows are old fashioned. Nowadays we use gas guns or shiny plastic that blows in the wind.'

Ken Tuckett, farmer from the other end of the village, came up to the bar.

'I still like scarecrows,' he said. 'Those gas guns make an awful noise and you can hear them all over the village.'

One or two of the regulars began to gather as whenever a new topic was discussed it was felt that a drinking man's duty was to offer an opinion.

'I remember scarecrows in the fields when I was a boy. We used to dress em up in all sorts of old clothes.' Mick Stanton was the official oldest inhabitant of the village. Aged eighty five he beat Foxy Sparrow by four years.

Foxy was in his usual seat by the fire. Not to be out done by Mick he said, 'There's some villages have a scarecrow festival. My cousin up in Lancashire has been to one at a village called Wray.'

Tom Heathcote joined in, 'In Tonbridge they have a scarecrow trail where people have to solve clues and follow the trail.'

'That's an idea,' said Richard. 'Kill two birds with one stone as it were. Let's have a scarecrow competition where anyone can make a scarecrow. We judge the best and they are the ones to go in your fields to scare the crows.'

*   *   *

Miss Wright, teacher at the school, heard of the competition from Jason Wilkins whose father had been in the pub that night. Jason was, as usual, very enthusiastic about the idea. He saw it as yet another thing for his gang, the Barrow Hill Boys.

The idea spread like wildfire around the village. All the children in Miss Wright's class wanted to make scarecrows and when Miss Tatt's class heard about it, they wanted to join in.

And so it was decided. The three farmers in the area, Jack Brownley, Ken Tuckett and Bert Ransom formed the committee and rules were drawn up. These were as follows:

Anyone in the village could make a scarecrow

They could be made in any shape with any materials

They could be placed anywhere in the village until they were judged

Judging would begin on Saturday two weeks hence.

Three scarecrows would be chosen as winners and placed, one in each farmer's field.

*   *   *

Betsy immediately wanted to make a scarecrow witch and Annabel agreed to help her but she pointed out a flaw in the rules.

'I don't know exactly how many fields there are around Happy End but there are a good many more than three. Why don't they put scarecrows up in every field and judge the winner as the ones that are best at keeping the birds away.'

Henry said that he would go to the pub that evening and suggest it to them. When he came back he was in a very merry mood.

'Too much to drink?' asked Annabel. 'Can't let you off on your own for a minute.'

Henry laughed. 'No it wasn't like that at all. I'm amused because they have put you on the committee and have asked if you will organise the event as they liked your idea.'

'Typical,' said Annabel. 'Put a group of men in a pub and they decide to get the women to do all the work.'

Inwardly she was pleased as she could see that this was another opportunity to increase the community spirit of the village with everyone working together.

* * *

And so it began. It wasn't only the children who wanted to take part, many adults decided they would have a go and cupboards were turned out to find old clothes and materials with which to make the scarecrows. Gradually a variety of figures began appearing round the village, mostly in people's gardens, until the first of May when they would be transferred to the fields.

It was quite alarming for visitors to the village at that time as anyone not knowing about the competition could round a corner and find themselves face to face with a straw giant, a prancing horse and all manner of inventions.

Jason and his gang managed to make a Dalek. Not quite like the Dr Who Daleks but near enough in shape and form. Jason had thought of putting Robin inside it so that he could point the gun at people and call out 'exterminate, exterminate,' but fortunately, although small, he wouldn't fit inside the carcase.

Betsy carried out her idea of a witch, the sort with a pointed hat and pointed chin dressed all in black and clutching a broomstick. Annabel gave her an old besom from the shed, which didn't have any magical properties.

At first, they put it at the entrance to the Garden Centre but then Henry decided to move it inside.

'If it scares me, it might scare the customers,' he said.

Happy End was a riot of colour as scarecrows of every shape and form appeared. Mrs Cooke even gave her old red flannel nightdress to one of the children to create a flaming dragon.

On the Wednesday, as agreed, the scarecrows were separated into three lots, one lot went to Jack Brownley's fields, one to Ken Tuckett's and the other to Bert Ransom. To avoid trampling the fields, Annabel arranged strict supervision for the placing of the scarecrows, making a note of the owners, and personally touring the fields making sure that the scarecrows were all properly in place.

'I'm fair puffed out,' she said collapsing into a chair that afternoon.

'I'll make the meal this evening, Mum,' Betsy offered.

'That's nice of you, Betsy love, but I can manage,'

she heaved herself out of the chair and went over to the window. 'At least all the scarecrows are out there on the fields and a fair sight they look.'

* * *

Judging was on Saturday which was in three days time.

'To give the birds' time to get used to them,' said Annabel.

Jack, Ken, Bert and Annabel would then go round the fields and do the judging. In the meantime word had gone round the neighbourhood and people from as far away as Chipping Sodbury, Gloucester and Stroud came to visit. Richard Brown was pleased as the Fox's Revenge did a roaring trade in food and drink. On the Thursday, poor Gladys, Richard's wife, was worked off her feet.

'And that Lucy Baxter isn't much help,' she said. 'Oh, she's alright at serving at the bar and making eyes at the men folk but when it comes to helping in the kitchen she's worse than useless.'

'We shall have to get someone else in to help you,' Richard was concerned. 'I'll ask Molly Pike. She's a good cook. At least that's what John Pike is always telling me.'

Molly was pleased to come and help as it meant a bit of extra money now that John had retired.

The village was a whirl of visitors. Strange shapes perched on sticks in the middle of the fields filled the area with a blaze of colour.

Annabel had carefully catalogued every scarecrow so

that when the judging was complete, the winner could be announced.

'I think I ought to do one last round before the judging begins tomorrow,' she said at breakfast on the Friday.

'You're acting like a mother hen over her chicks with these scarecrows,' said Henry between mouthfuls of cornflakes. 'Leave it be and go round with the judging tomorrow.'

'I've just got this feeling that something isn't right,' she said.

'Your feelings are usually right,' he said. 'If you want to wear yourself out again, then go ahead.'

'I'll come with you, Mum,' said Betsy.

It was early so not many people were about but when they got to the first field, they were surprised to find all the scarecrows lying in the mud. It had rained that night but as Annabel pointed out. 'That shouldn't be enough to flatten them like this and there was no wind to speak of.'

Annabel was furious. 'Someone has done this,' she said. 'All the work that people have put in and now it is ruined.'

They quickly toured the other fields and were relieved to find that the rest of the scarecrows were in safely in place. It was just this one field.

'What are we going to do, Mum,' asked Betsy.

'Find the culprit and fix the problem,' she said. 'Let's go back home.'

After they had gone from the ruined field, a scarecrow picked itself up and looked around. 'That was some night,' it said.

*　*　*

Annabel went straight to her workroom and her crystal. Focussing on the flattened field, she was surprised to see that one scarecrow was still standing.

'That wasn't there this morning,' she said to Betsy who was leaning over her shoulder.

'It's moving,' said Betsy.

'That's not a scarecrow,' said Annabel. 'It's a human being and a pretty disreputable one at that. We are going to have to go back but first let's revive the scarecrows in that field.' She concentrated on a spell and Betsy could see all six of the scarecrows mounted back on their sticks surrounding the strange human being dressed like a conventional scarecrow.

'Let's go,' Annabel put the crystal back in the cupboard covering it with a cloth.

They arrived back at the field to find that a crowd had gathered watching what was apparently a scarecrow fighting all the other scarecrows and knocking them over.

'Stop that,' Annabel called out and made her way very gingerly out to the middle of the field. The figure stopped fighting and stood looking at her.

'And who might you be madam?' it asked. It was dressed just like a scarecrow with an old dress coat buttoned up at the front with tails flapping at the back. Its trousers, originally black, were green with age and like a real scarecrow, straw was coming out of its sleeves and boots.

'Stop knocking those scarecrows about and come over here,' Annabel commanded.

She led him over to the far side of the field where he collapsed onto the grassy bank.

'Who are you?' she asked.

The figure attempted to rise without success. 'Augustus Jennings-Smythe at your service.' It waved a brown paper-clad bottle.

'And you madam?'

'Never mind who I am,' Annabel snapped. 'What were you doing knocking over these scarecrows?'

Augustus put the bottle down and heaved himself up on his elbow.

'Is that what they are. I was a little inebriated last night.' He indicated the bottle.

'I wandered into this field to find a place to sleep for the night and found myself surrounded by all manner of fearsome creatures. I did the only thing I could, I fought each and every one of them, knocking them down. When I woke up this morning I thought it was a dream as they were all standing up again and surrounding me.'

Annabel smiled. 'Let's just say I put them back up again before you woke. But what are you doing here and why are you dressed like a scarecrow?'

Augustus smoothed the front of his dress coat. 'Gentleman of the road, that what I am. Any old clothes welcome. Do you have some?'

'Later, maybe,' said Annabel, 'but what about the straw?'

'Don't you know?' asked Augustus. 'Finest thing known to man for insulation. Cold night, so I stuffed it into my clothes.'

'Come on,' said Annabel. 'Let's get you out of this field and put some food inside you.' She helped him up and led him through the crowd.

As they walked back down the village she could hear comments from passers by.

'They have really gone to town with this scarecrow competition.'

'Look, a real live scarecrow, what a laugh.'

'They think you are part of the competition,' said Annabel. 'That gives me an idea.'

Seated in Annabel's kitchen, eating a hearty breakfast as though he hadn't eaten for a week, Augustus told the story of how he became, what he insisted on calling, 'a gentleman of the road.'

'I was something in the City,' he said. 'Lots of money and then the crash. Finances down the drain. Destitute. Love travelling but had to do it on the cheap. Walk, get lifts, sleep rough. Just been walking the Stroud valley. Beautiful area, not nice in the rain but better weather coming. Got a lift to Cirencester and found my way here. Looked for a barn to sleep in but, unusual for me, got inebriated and the rest you know.'

Annabel took a careful look at him. He might be dressed oddly, she thought, but he is a tall well-mannered man with a thin but intelligent face and he speaks well.

'I want you to do something for me,' she said.

'Anything, dear lady,'

Annabel told him her idea and suggested that he rest up in one of the old potting sheds. Henry was a bit surprised when he was introduced, but as usual, fell in with Annabel's schemes.

Augustus spent the morning sleeping, only waking when Annabel took him some food. In the afternoon she went with him to see Jack Brownley and explain her idea.

* * *

Saturday dawned, and it was time for the judging. At nine o'clock sharp, there was the sound of a tractor driving down towards the Fox's Revenge. It was towing a decorated cart driven by Augustus wearing an old top hat added to his costume. Jack Brownley was already seated in the cart and at the pub they picked up Ken, Bert and Annabel.

Augustus' job was to drive them round the fields to judge the scarecrows. At nine o'clock, there were not many visitors about but those that were raised a cheer as the spectacle went by.

The original idea had been to judge the scarecrows by the number of birds they scared away but Saturday mornings may be resting times for birds, or maybe the sound of the tractor drove them away. In any event, the fields seemed clear of birds.

'We shall just have to judge them on merit,' said Jack

and the others agreed.

'In the end they selected the three winners, the dragon made from Mrs Cooke's nightgown, the Dalek made by the Barrow Hill Boys, and a rather nice tableau depicting a scene from the wizard of Oz with Dorothy, the tin man and the cowardly lion, made by pupils from Miss Wright's form at the school. Betsy was disappointed that her witch hadn't won but as Annabel pointed out, it wouldn't be fair if relatives of the judges were to win and in any case it would make a nice bird scarer for the Garden Centre.

All the winners were awarded a certificate and everyone's scarecrows were to be kept in the fields until the danger from the birds had passed.

The judges, along with Augustus, went to the pub to have a celebratory lunch in Richard's private room and during the meal, Jack Brownley offered Augustus a job.

'I need another farmhand,' he said. 'I can offer you accommodation in an old cottage on the farm. What do you say?'

Augustus raised his tankard and said, 'As long as you don't expect me to stand in the middle of a field and scare birds, I'm your man.'

8

Australian Adventure

Emilina Twitchett was in distress. Annabel sat her down and brought her a cup of tea.

'What's the matter, my love?' she said.

Emilina gulped the hot tea, and then set it aside. 'It's Tom my eldest boy who lives in Australia. You remember you told me I would be getting a letter from him and that he would come over to see me, bringing his new wife?'

'Yes, I saw it in the crystal,' said Annabel.

'Well, I did get a letter and he told me that he had married and was coming back to this country with his wife. They were supposed to arrive and come down to see me two weeks ago but they haven't phoned or contacted me. I'm worried about what might have happened to them.'

'Don't you have their phone number?' asked Betsy.

'I do and I have tried to telephone but there was no

answer. I think I used the right number. I didn't like to try again as overseas calls are so expensive.'

'That might just mean that they are on the way and have been delayed for some reason,' said Betsy.

Annabel put on her soothing voice. 'I'm sure everything is all right but if you like I could take a look in the crystal.'

'Would you Annabel. I'd be so grateful.'

'I shall need something of your son's to focus on. Do you have anything with you?'

Emilina fumbled with the locket around her neck. 'I've got this picture of him when he was a boy. Would that do?'

'Come on into the workroom.' Annabel led the way, taking her crystal ball out of the cupboard. 'Sit down and let's see.'

Emilina sat down obediently while Annabel took the locket and concentrated on the crystal.

Eventually she sat back.

'Nothing is coming through at all,' she said. 'I shall have to try later. You go home and don't worry. I will be in touch as soon as I have some news. If you hear anything, let me know. Can I keep the locket for now? You had better let me have his address as well.'

'He lives in Perth, I'll write the address down for you,' said Emilina tearful but momentarily reassured. She left, leaving Annabel looking at the crystal.

It hasn't failed me before like this, she thought. She tried again but without success.

Later she discussed it with Henry and Betsy. 'I can't

understand it,' she said. 'I should have been able to see something but it was all just a blank.'

'Perhaps you are losing your powers,' said Henry.

'Thank you very much, Mr Witchell.'

'I'm sure its not that, Mum,' said Betsy. 'There must be some other reason.'

'Yes, but what?' asked Annabel.

'Why not look at it another way,' said Betsy. 'If you can't get anything out of the crystal why not use more conventional methods.'

'Of course, the telephone. I get so bound up with witchery that I forget that modern communications make the world a much smaller place.'

'I wasn't thinking of the telephone. Emilina has already tried that. I was thinking of computers,' said Betsy.

'Computers?' said Annabel.

'Using a computer you can reach across the world in minutes,'

'I've heard of this, but who has got a computer?' asked Annabel.

'Mr Stanton has one,' said Betsy. 'I was going to see him to ask about them. I might need one for my university studies.'

Annabel was always keen to add to her knowledge so they made an appointment to see Mick Stanton the next day. What surprised Annabel was that Mick Stanton who was eighty-five years old should be interested in modern technology.

'Ah, well you see, Annabel,' he said when they arrived at his tiny cottage, 'My son who is now in Australia got me interested and you know how long a letter takes to reach foreign parts. Well, with my computer I can send an email and get a reply the same day. Come into my den and I'll show you.' He led the way into the small back room crowded with equipment.

'I was a radio ham in the old days when, with my wireless transmitter, I spent hours at night talking to people all over the world much to the disgust of my dear wife, God rest her soul. She's been gone these twenty long years. You can see how easy it was to switch to this modern technology, which means I can communicate with my son and I also have friends all across the world. You probably haven't come across Twitter, Bebo, Facebook and all these social networks but believe me they are wonderful for us old folk stuck in our homes without anyone to talk to, but I mustn't ramble on. What can I do for you?'

'It's a whole new world for me,' said Annabel. 'I'd better let Betsy explain.'

'Best go back into the sitting room,' said Mick. 'There's no room to move in here.'

When they were settled, Betsy explained that Mrs Twitchett's son Tom was supposed to be bringing his new bride over from Australia to Happy End but was two weeks overdue.

'We wondered if you could get in touch with someone over there to find out what was happening,' said Annabel.

'Australia is a big place,' said Mick. 'Whereabouts is her son located?'

'Perth,' said Annabel. 'Here is the address of their apartment.' She handed him a piece of paper.

'My son is in Adelaide but I do know someone in Perth,' said Mick. 'I can look up his email address.'

He went back into his den and brought back a laptop computer.

'This is a portable computer,' he explained putting it on the small table by his chair. 'It's linked to the Internet by a WiFi transmitter. We'll just wait until it warms up.'

Annabel was fascinated. Betsy was watching with great interest.

After a few minutes, he was able to find the email address in his address book.

'It might be an idea,' he said, 'to just see how big Perth is, then we shall know what we are dealing with.' He typed in *Wikipedia*.

'This is a free encyclopedia,' he explained. ' Anyone can write articles for it. It claims to be one of the largest reference web sites. Here's the entry for Perth.'

On the screen appeared a map of the city and a long account.

'It says that Perth is the largest city in Western Australia with a population of around one and a half million people. There's a lot more about it being founded in 1829 by Captain James Stirling but we don't need to bother with that.'

'See, Mum, how useful this will be for my university

studies,' said Betsy.

'I can see that,' said Annabel, 'but how expensive are these things?'

'They have come down a lot,' said Mick. 'There's a very good computer shop in Barrow Magna kept by Arnold Jackson. If you go and see him, mention my name. He should give you a good deal. Let's get back to your problem. What's the plan?'

They discussed how they should approach the problem and decided that Mick would send his friend, Tony, a message asking if he knew anyone in the area where Tom Twitchett lived. If he did then he would ask if they could go round to see what had happened. Otherwise, it would mean contacting the local police station.

As luck would have it, Mick's friend Tony Wasson was online and almost immediately they received a reply.

'You've got to remember that although it's eleven o'clock here, it's six o'clock in the evening in Perth.'

'Halfway around the world and you get a reply as quickly as that,' said Annabel. 'That almost beats magic.'

Mick smiled. 'It's not always as easy as this,' he said. 'Let's read what he has to say.'

It turned out that Tony lived not far from Tom Twitchett's address and was prepared to go round next day to see what he could find out.

*   *   *

Next day, Annabel and Betsy were back at Mick Stanton's cottage. He greeted them with a serious look.

'Tony went round to Mr Twitchett's apartment this morning which you must remember was our last night , it's now five o clock in the afternoon over there.'

'What did he find out?' asked Betsy.

'Nothing good I'm afraid,' said Mick. 'Excuse me if I sit down, my rheumatics is playing me up something terrible this morning. Sit yourselves down and I'll tell you all about it.'

This is what he told them based on the long email that he had received.

Two months ago, Tom Twitchett and Ann his new wife had moved into their new apartment and had happily spent the time making it into their nest. They reserved a room for the nursery but before they started a family, Tom wanted to take Ann to meet his mother in England. Tom arranged a two-week holiday from his firm. They planned the trip. Tom wrote to his mother and everything was set for them to fly over. The day before they were due to fly, Tom came home from work to find that Ann was missing. At first, he thought that she was out shopping but as evening set in, he began to worry.

One of his neighbours in the apartment block told him that they had seen a car draw up and a man pushing a struggling figure into the car. Tom informed the police and had spent most of his time at the police station. He had managed to ring the airline who had been sympathetic and had agreed to refund the tickets subject to a service charge.

He was so distraught that he forgot to phone his mother. The police had no leads other than the neighbour's statement and Tom didn't know what to do. When Tony had arrived that morning, he poured the whole story out to him. He had now phoned his mother just telling her that they had been delayed and that he would be in touch as soon as he could.

'She will know that something is wrong from his tone of voice,' said Annabel. 'I must go and comfort her and then we need to think about what to do.'

'I don't know what you can do from this distance,' said Mick.

Annabel looked at him.

'You'd be surprised,' she said.

*　　*　　*

After going to see Emilina Twitchett and reassuring her that they would do everything they could to help, she went home to discuss with Henry and Betsy what action to take.

'I think I am going to have to go over there,' she said. 'The crystal didn't work at this distance and if I get to Tom's address I am sure I can find out what happened.'

Betsy looked alarmed. 'Are you going to go out-of-the-body or do you mean you will catch a plane or a boat?' she asked.

'Out-of-the-body is no good in this case. I need a physical presence but real travel would take too long. I'm going to have to get there by magic.'

'But, Mum I know you can do short hops, but this is halfway round the world.'

'I'll just have to concentrate hard then, won't I?'

Henry sat back in his chair. 'I can't stop you when your mind is made up but don't you think it's dangerous attempting to project yourself all that way?'

'Not if I'm careful,' she said, 'but if you two can think of a better idea?'

And so it was agreed that Annabel would go that night so that she arrived in Perth the next morning due to the seven hour time difference.

✳ ✳ ✳

Tom Twitchett lived in an apartment block in Victory Park. It was an old suburb in the Southern area of Perth. Annabel arrived in the street outside Tom's block. She had left home at midnight and since transporting herself was almost instantaneous, she arrived at about seven in the morning. It was a leafy suburb and Annabel had a nice feeling about it. There were quite a number of people moving about, both young and old. The architecture was mixed. Modern apartment blocks were right up against older houses that had seen better times. Tom's block was one of the older ones and Annabel reasoned probably better built than the gleaming steel and concrete blocks. She went up to the second floor after announcing herself as a friend of his mother on the security phone at street level.

Tom opened the door and invited her in. He was a tall fair-haired man casually dressed in slacks and a shirt, unshaven and looking worried.

When she explained that she had come from England to help, he took a good look at her. What he saw was a typical farmer's wife, jolly, round-faced with blue eyes that seemed to bore right through him.

How can you help, he thought to himself but what he said was, 'How did you get here so quickly?'

'Never mind about that,' Annabel said briskly. 'The important thing is to find out what has happened to your new wife.'

She went into the kitchen making a cup of tea for them both, noting the dirty dishes and generally untidiness. She sat Tom down and soon had the whole story from him. In essence, it was the same story that she had heard from Mick Stanton but it was obvious that he wanted to go over the whole thing again in his mind. The police he said had no clues. The only information was that of the neighbour who had seen the struggle. What could he do?

'It's more what I can do, my lad,' said Annabel. 'Why don't you go out and get a bit of fresh air while I see what I can see.'

Without knowing why he should trust a strange woman that he had just met, Tom found himself putting his coat on and heading out of the door.

'Come back in about half an hour,' Annabel called.

Annabel then sat down and concentrated her thoughts.

After a while, the scene began to take shape. There was Ann, a slender young woman sitting at the table when there was a knock at the door. She opened it and a man thrust his way into the room. She seemed to know him as when he grasped her arm roughly she called out, 'Stop it Grier.'

He pulled her to him and said, 'You're mine. I'm not going to let you go.'

He then dragged her from the room and there were sounds of a struggle on the stairs.

Annabel gradually came back to consciousness, went to the kitchen and poured herself another cup of tea. So that's the way of it, she thought.

When Tom came back, she asked him for a sheet of paper. Turning her back on him so that he couldn't see what she was doing she quickly impressed a head and shoulders picture of the man on to the paper. She showed it to Tom.

'That's the man that took your wife,' she said.

'But that's Grier Matson,' said Tom, 'How did you do that?'

Annabel held him with her eyes, 'I'm able to see things that others can't,' she said.

Tom took the paper in his hand and looked closely at it. 'If that is the man who took Ann then I know why. She told me about him. Before we met she was engaged to this man but she found out that he had been married before and his wife had divorced him for cruelty. At first, he was very attentive to her but fortunately, she began to see through him and broke their engagement. She told me that he had pestered her for a while after that but then she met me and we fell in love.'

'The question is what to do next,' said Annabel. 'Do we go to the police with this or would you like me to find her for you?'

'Can you do that?' he asked.

Annabel smiled. 'Yes, I can and in any case I don't think the police would believe the word of someone who has just popped into your life, would they?'

'It does seem fantastic,' said Tom. 'I feel as if I am in the middle of a nightmare, but what can you do?'

'Just leave it to me. Stay here and I'll be back as soon as I can.' She went into the kitchen and shut the door.

'But,' said Tom opening the kitchen door. 'What …'

Annabel had gone and poor Tom was left feeling even more disoriented.

Using the picture, she projected herself to where Grier Matson was holding Ann. She arrived in a darkened room where she could make out a figure tied to a chair. It was Ann. She untied her bonds and helped her get up. At that moment, the lock in the door turned and Grier Matson entered the room, putting the light on.

'What the …,' he exclaimed seeing before him Ann hugging what he thought was a little old lady.

He began to advance into the room.

'I don't know how you got in here,' he said, 'but you can just get out the same way.'

'We both can,' said Annabel. 'First, however, you need to be taught a lesson.'

Grier Matson made as if to grab Ann but she evaded him so he turned his attention to Annabel. He went to hit her but then to his astonishment found that with fist outstretched he couldn't move. Annabel gave him a push and he fell on to a chair. She stood over him.

'The spell will wear off in an hour but remember what I am about to tell you. This time you won't be in trouble with the police but if you ever bother Ann again you will find that you have me to deal with. Just in case that doesn't convince you perhaps this will,' and she looked deep into his eyes.

What Grier Matson saw was not a cheerful countrywoman but a towering monstrosity with horns, glaring mad red eyes, slavering fangs, and talons reaching to tear his heart out. He couldn't move a muscle but inside he could feel his heart beating faster. He was terrified.

Annabel broke the link and holding Ann's hand transported them back to Tom's apartment.

Tom had fallen asleep in a chair but on their arrival started up.

'Ann,' he clasped her firmly. 'Where have you been?'

'It's a long story,' she said turning to Annabel. 'How can I thank you for rescuing me. I don't even know who you are?'

'I'm a friend of Tom's mother,' said Annabel. 'Now I must think about getting home as my family will be worried about me. Tell Tom all about it and I shall look forward to seeing you soon in Happy End.'

'How will you get back?' asked Tom.

'Like this,' said Annabel and she faded into nothingness leaving Tom and Ann looking at the space where she had been.

9

The Parish Magazine

'I have always wanted to start a Parish Magazine.' The Reverend Alistair Harding waved his piece of toast.

His wife Victoria listened attentively as usual.

'I'm surprised it has taken you so long,' she said.

'It was Tom and Ann who made me think about it,' he said.

Tom Twitchett had brought his new wife Ann over from Australia to meet his mother Emilina and as churchgoers they had been in Sunday's congregation. They had also been to see Annabel to thank her for her help in the rescue of Ann.

'A nice young couple,' said Alistair. 'They were telling me about their church magazine. They told me it was quite a community thing and convinced me that we ought to have one.'

'You have had that sheet you leave in the church with all the times on it. What would a parish magazine consist of?' she asked.

'We could publish it once a month and as well as the church items it could have articles and reports on local activities, we could invite all the clubs and societies to write a piece.'

'I didn't know we had many clubs in Happy End. They mostly seem to be in Barrow Magna.'

'That's true but let us start small and see where it leads. It won't be more than a couple of folded A4 sheets at first and it will have to be free delivery to all households in the village.' Alistair began to wax enthusiastic.

'I hate to bring you down to earth,' she said, 'but who is going to produce it and how will you pay for it if it's free to everyone.'

'Good question,' said Alistair. 'I'll have to think about that but it's a good idea and I want to do it.'

He did think about it and, after talking again to Tom and Ann, contacted Mick Stanton the village's oldest inhabitant who had played a part in the initial stages of Ann's rescue. Mick was all set up with computers and printers and so was the ideal person to type the magazine for the vicar.

He readily agreed. 'No charge of course, Vicar. I would be pleased to do it.'

Alistair then went to see John Perry, the local printers in Barrow Magna, who gave him a quote for printing a hundred and fifty copies, three sheets of A4 folded and stapled.

'That gives you twelve A5 size pages,' he said. 'Will that be enough?'

'More than enough,' said Alistair. 'All I have to do now is find enough material to fill it, find a way to pay for it and get someone to distribute it.'

The money and distribution came in an unexpected way. He was talking to Colonel Blackley about it. When he told him how much it would cost, the Colonel got out his chequebook and wrote out a cheque for twice that amount.

'That will keep you going for two issues,' he said, 'and I'm sure that Beryl would help with the distribution.'

Beryl Blackburn was the young girl who went in every day and 'did for him' as she put it. Previously Annabel had helped Colonel Trevor Blackley to get rid of two scheming servants, Bert Scoggins and Freda Wilkins, by sending them up to Edinburgh. The Colonel having learnt his lesson, now used only local labour. Beryl did the housework and he had approached Mollie Pike to cook for him.

Alistair Harding was delighted with the cheque and after asking Beryl and getting her agreement, went back to the vicarage to discuss possible content with his wife.

'There are all the usual church items,' he said. 'Then, if he would agree, Henry Witchell could do a gardening column.'

At that point, his creativity dried up but his wife suggested that an announcement from the pulpit on Sunday ought to bring in some ideas.

His announcement didn't bring any immediate results but it started people thinking. The Pettit sisters thought they might write something on collecting glassware and pottery. Their house was awash with things they had accumulated over the years. Henry Witchell agreed to do a gardening column and Tommy Tucker suggested a piece on art, although he wasn't sure on what aspect of it. Miss Tatt and Miss Wright agreed to do a School Report.

'Everyone has been most co-operative,' Alistair told Victoria. 'I asked Mollie Pike if she would write out some recipes for us but she said she had never written anything in her life, after school that is, so I didn't press her.'

'Why don't I talk to her and write out recipes for her?' Victoria asked.

'That's a good idea. I think with a useful information section giving times for surgery, Post Office times and things like that, we should have plenty to fill the first issue.'

'Don't forget a Letters to the Editor section. People might like to write in. What about advertising? Some local firms might pay to have an advertisement in the magazine.'

'I don't think paid advertising should be in a church magazine do you?' he asked.

'To be honest,' said Victoria, 'it's beginning to look more like a village magazine than a church one. You might consider paid advertisements as a way to financing future issues.'

'Let's get the first issue out and then we'll see,' he said and so he set to work to collect the material and get it to Mick Stanton.

In the end, he had more than enough to fill the first issue. Annabel had suggested a piece on herbal medicines but he had to tell her that he did not have room for it in this issue but would consider it later.

'The problems of being an editor,' he said to Victoria. 'You can never satisfy everyone. Mabel Todd approached me the other day and wanted to do a chatty column but I had to turn her down.'

'At least you can launch the first issue,' Victoria said. 'I take it you haven't had any letters to the Editor yet?'

'No, I shall invite them in my editorial for the next issue.'

'Don't make your editorial too much like a sermon,' his wife warned.

He laughed. 'Don't worry, you shall read it before it goes into print.'

* * *

All went well except for the Pettit sisters' article which had photographs in it.

'We can only use line drawings at present,' he told them. 'I'll ask Tommy Tucker if he can redraw them for you.'

Rosemary Pettit looked disappointed. 'That will not be the same,' she said. 'However, you are the editor.'

'Sorry,' said Alistair. 'I'll talk to the printer and see what we can do next time.'

Tommy Tucker agreed immediately and very quickly produced the drawings.

At last, everything was given to Mick Stanton and he produced the final version for the printer.

'John Perry has done an excellent job,' Alistair told his wife, showing her a copy.

'I like the front page,' his wife said. 'Did Tommy do the drawing of the church for you.'

'Yes, without me asking him. He said he would like to design the cover and he has done an excellent job. Now all we have to do is get it distributed.'

He took the copies up to the Manor and gave them to Beryl Blackburn who was working in the kitchen with Mollie Pike.

'Ooh, that's nice,' said Beryl. 'Look Mollie. I'll take it round the village tomorrow when I get off work.' She put the pile of magazines carefully on a side table.

* * *

Next day a copy of the magazine dropped through Annabel's letterbox. Henry had just come in.

'Let's have a look ,' he said. 'See how my article has come out.'

He leafed through the pages. 'Hello, what this?'

He held up a sheet of paper inserted into the magazine pages.

'Look,' he said holding it out. 'It's headed Gossip Column and there's a letter about Colonel Blackley.'

Annabel took the sheet and read it out. 'It has come to our attention that Colonel Blackley has been seen with Mrs Oakley.'

'She's the widow up at the new houses,' said Annabel.

'Go on,' said Henry.

'Has been seen with Mrs Oakley. Is something going on between them?'

'I can't read the rest of it,' she said. 'This is a poison pen letter. How on earth did it get into the magazine?'

All over Happy End, people were picking up the magazine and finding the badly printed sheet that had been inserted into it. The magazine itself was largely ignored.

The one person who mattered, Patricia Oakley, didn't open her magazine until after coffee that morning. She had moved into the village about a month ago but, as yet, had not made any real friends although as usual the Pettit sisters had paid her a visit. If she had made friends all sorts of people would have rung her up to tell her what had happened but as no-one really knew her they didn't dare.

She opened the magazine and the extra sheet fell on the floor where it stayed while she read the rest of the magazine.

A very good publication, she thought, I must congratulate the vicar. Seeing the extra page on the floor, she picked it up and was going to consign it to the waste paper basket when she caught sight of her name and she read on.

'Well, really' she exclaimed aloud. 'Who is this Colonel Blackley? What rubbish!'

She was so incensed that she looked up the Colonel's phone number and was going to ring him when the phone rang. It was the Colonel.

'My dear lady,' he began hesitatingly. 'My dear lady, I hardly know how to begin. Have you read the scurrilous letter in the magazine?'

'I have,' she said. 'I find it most offensive. I didn't think a quiet village like this one would harbour such a poisonous letter writer.'

'It's all untrue, of course,' said the Colonel. 'Since we haven't met, may I call on you to apologise in person.'

Although she was annoyed, the Colonel's voice sounded nice and friendly so she invited him to tea that afternoon.

'After all,' she said to herself, 'all the village will think there is something between us after seeing this letter so let's give them something to think about.'

Patricia Oakley was a very attractive woman in her forties who, with her husband, a banker, had enjoyed a life of parties and theatres with a wide circle of friends in London. Widowed a year ago she had moved to Happy End 'to start a new life' although her friends thought she was mad to bury herself in the country where 'nothing ever happens, my dear'.

She had been so busy putting her home in order that she had done little socialising apart from church going and visits to the Post Office Stores. She now intended to change that and it looked as if this poison pen letter was actually a gift from heaven to begin to meet interesting people.

The Colonel arrived, and she served him tea, cake and scones. Mrs Oakley was an excellent cook and had spent the most of the morning baking. Their meeting was an immediate success. They laughed over the stupid letter and discovered that they had interests in common. They both enjoyed the theatre, books, and walking.

'Although I shall have to give up the theatre,' she said.

'Not a bit of it,' said the Colonel. 'Often go up to London to see a show. I'm thinking of going to see Rattigan's *Separate Tables*. It's on at the National. Why don't you come with me?'

'But how would we get there?' Patricia thought that this was rather forward of the Colonel but, well, nothing venture nothing gain.

'Have an arrangement with a man in Barrow Magna, runs the local taxi firm. He takes me up, waits and brings me back. Gives me a special rate as I'm a regular of his.'

'I'd love to come, let's fix a date, but I suppose we should get back to the subject of this awful letter. Oughtn't we to do something about it Colonel?'

'I'll talk to the vicar. See if he can account for it,' said the Colonel. 'By the way, call me Trevor, my friends call me Teddy.'

'And I'm Pat,' she said. They solemnly shook hands.

* * *

The Colonel did have a word with the vicar but Alistair was at a loss to explain it.

'It wasn't there when I gave the magazines to Beryl for distribution,' he said. 'Someone must have slipped it in afterwards. Do you want me to pursue the matter?'

'Actually no harm done,' said the Colonel. 'I've now met the lady concerned and she is a charming person. I think perhaps things are best left alone.'

When Alistair spoke to Victoria about it, he admitted to being disturbed. 'I know the Colonel said to leave it but someone used the magazine for a bad purpose. I can't get that out of my mind.'

'Why don't you ask Annabel Witchell about it,' she said. 'She knows everyone in the village and I'm sure that she could put her finger on the culprit.'

So Alistair went to have a word with Annabel.

'I would hate to think that we have a poison pen writer in our midst,' he said. 'I cannot believe that there is anyone in the village that malicious.'

'You would be surprised, vicar. These small villages often breed resentment and envy. I'll have a think about this and get back to you if I find something.'

Alistair knew something of Annabel's methods and was content to let it go at that.

*　*　*

Annabel did think about it and realised that the most obvious culprit was Beryl Blackburn as she had the magazines the day before and could have inserted the sheet before distributing them. She went up to the Manor next day.

'Oh no, I wouldn't do a thing like that,' Beryl said, when questioned. 'Why would I? The Colonel is a nice gentleman.

I wouldn't want to do anything to harm him.'

Annabel held Beryl with her eyes and asked her again but it was the same answer.

'Do you know how it might have happened,' she asked, still keeping Beryl held with a hypnotic stare.

'I don't know,' said Beryl. 'I left the magazines in the kitchen that night and collected them next day so that I could bring a basket to put them in and take them round the village early before I started work.'

'So the culprit must have somehow come into the kitchen overnight and inserted the extra page,' said Annabel thoughtfully. 'Thank you, Beryl, I shall have to ask the Colonel who else has access to this room.'

When she asked Colonel Blackley he looked rather embarrassed and said 'Apart from Beryl and Mrs Pike of course no-one. Certainly not after they have gone.'

Annabel sensed that the Colonel was holding something back. She didn't like to probe his mind as she had Beryl's so she said, 'You're hiding something. What is it.'

He looked even more embarrassed and said, 'Let me show you something.'

He led the way upstairs to one of the rooms on the second floor.

'Take a look in there,' he said.

He led Annabel into the room which was obviously some sort of junk storage room but there at one side was a desk with a typewriter and an old Roneo duplicating machine.

Annabel went over to the duplicator. 'I haven't seen one of these in years,' she said. Then she noticed some crumpled up pages in the nearby wastepaper basket. She took one out and opened it.

'So that was how it was done,' she said. 'But who did it?'

Colonel Blackley turned a slight tinge of pink. 'I did,' he said.

'But why?' she asked.

'I think you had better come back downstairs and I will tell you,' he said.

By the time they had reached the sitting room, he had regained his composure.

'You know my history,' he said. After I lost my wife I had those rascally servants in the house and thank goodness you helped me to get rid of them. Well, I miss my wife and I thought that there would be no-one who could ever replace her until I met Patricia Oakley. It was only a chance meeting in the Post Office Stores but it was love at first sight.'

'That still doesn't explain why you wrote a poison pen letter about yourself,' said Annabel.

'You see, I am a very shy person and I couldn't bring myself to make overtures to her so I hit on the idea of accusing myself of being involved with her. This gave me a chance to meet her and apologise and it worked. I'm taking her to the theatre and hopefully our friendship will blossom.'

Annabel looked at him with amusement. 'It seems a very odd way to start a relationship and what about the rest of the village? Everyone has seen the letter which now I think about it was really quite mild as poison pen letters go.'

'Can't we just leave it as it is?' asked the Colonel. 'Does everyone have to know the truth? At the moment they think I am involved with her and I hope I shall be.'

'I think I should tell the vicar as it is his magazine which you used,' said Annabel, 'but I don't see that it needs to go any further.'

Annabel did tell the vicar and he agreed not to divulge it to anyone.

'Not even my wife,' he said. 'Although she would love to know.'

The same happened with Henry. He asked Annabel if she had solved the mystery and she said enigmatically, 'Some things are best left alone.'

Art and Craft

'They are threatening to expose me to the village.'

Tommy Tucker had come to Annabel with his tale of woe as previously she had helped him find a new life for himself in the village after being accused of a murder that he didn't commit.

He explained. 'Two men came to my caravan late last night and told me that they knew all about me and that unless I did what they said, they would tell the whole village about the double life of Jason Tarbury and Tommy Tucker and that I had been accused of murder.'

'It only needs a whisper of something like that to run round the village like wildfire,' said Annabel thoughtfully. 'What did they want?'

'They said that they were acting for someone whose valuable painting had been stolen by thieves and they had been commissioned to recover it. Apparently the thief lives in a large house nearby but he and his family were abroad for two weeks and this was an ideal time for them to recover the painting and replace it with a copy. They want me to paint the copy.'

'Sounds fishy to me,' said Annabel. 'It looks as if they are planning to steal someone's painting and sell it.'

'That's what I thought, but what can I do? I enjoy living in this village and I want it to go on.'

'We could tell the Pettit sisters the whole story. They would soon spread it round the village and then you would have nothing to fear from these men.'

Tommy wriggled uncomfortably. 'No, I can't do that. It would be too painful. I've come to see if you can help. They are coming back tonight to get my answer.'

Annabel sat and thought. The glimmering of an idea came to her.

'How do you know you can copy it?' she asked.

'I can copy anything,' said Tommy proudly. 'In any case they showed me a print of the picture. It looks like an early Monet, one of his Haystack series. He was fascinated by the play of light on things under different weather conditions. If this is the painting they are going to steal it really is quite valuable.'

'In that case, go home and when they come, tell them you will do it but say that you need paying as well as their guarantee of silence about your past. That makes it more believable.'

'But,' said Tommy. 'You're suggesting that I make myself accessory to a theft?'

'It won't be a theft when I've finished with it,' said Annabel. 'Do what I say and come back tomorrow to report progress.'

That evening after dinner, Annabel retired to her room to go out-of-the-body so that she could follow the thieves. Henry and Betsy never got used to this although Betsy had practised it herself and indeed asked if she could go as well, but Annabel refused.

'Not this time, young lady. I want to see what they are up to and I will be quicker on my own. Next time, may be.'

With that, Betsy had to be content.

Annabel was soon out of her body and quickly over to Tommy Tucker's caravan just in time to follow two shadowy figures into their car. Annabel settled herself comfortably into the back seat as they drove off. She listened while they discussed tactics and she learnt that their target was Hinchcombe Hall, just across the border in Wiltshire. She also found out that they had a buyer in France who was willing to take the painting, no questions asked. She did not follow them into the house but travelled back with them after they had taken the picture, concealing it in the boot of the car. To her surprise she found that their destination was the Fox's Revenge where they were obviously staying the night and going to take the painting to Tommy Tucker next day.

*   *   *

Tommy came to see her next morning and reported that they had agreed to pay him a thousand pounds. Five hundred in advance, and five hundred on delivery.

'They must want it badly,' said Annabel.

'Its real worth is many hundred's of thousands more than that,' he said. 'The only problem is they want the copy by Sunday at the latest.'

'What about the paint,' asked Annabel. 'Surely an expert would be able to tell that the pigments are modern?'

'As far as I know, it will be in the house with the rest of the pictures. If the owners don't suspect anything it will just hang there.'

'In any case I can help you with that,' said Annabel, 'but I want you to paint two copies. Can you do it in the time?'

'I can,' said Tommy, 'but why?'

'This is my idea,' she said.

Annabel talked to Tommy for a long time about paints and pigments then she gave him his final instructions and he set off back to his caravan.

* * *

Annabel could hardly wait until the weekend but Saturday eventually dawned.

'Can I come with you to see the painting?' asked Betsy.

'Yes, my love, I want to go over early just in case those men turn up today instead of on Sunday.'

They went down to the caravan and were greeted by a

triumphant Tommy wearing a paint spattered smock.

'I've finished,' he said. 'Come and look.'

They went into the caravan and there were three paintings lined up side by side.

It was obvious which one was the original as the copies shone with their fresh paint.

'Just wait for me outside Betsy. Take Tommy with you as I have to do a little magic.'

After a short while, Annabel came out.

'Come and look now,' she said.

They went back in and there were the three paintings but now they all looked exactly alike.

'Which is the original?' she asked.

'I'm blowed if I know,' said Tommy. 'Do you know Betsy.'

'That one,' she said pointing.

'Not far off but it's this one,' Annabel pointed to the middle of the three. 'I marked it before I went to work on them. I doubt now if anyone can tell them apart.'

Annabel made sure that Tommy understood his final instructions, then packing the original painting in brown paper she gave it to Betsy to carry home.

Betsy was nervous about carrying it. 'What happens if someone sees us?' she asked.

'Don't worry, I'm putting a cloak of invisibility on it so no-one will see anything.'

With Betsy reassured they set off back to the Garden Centre.

* * *

Next day Tommy reported that all had gone well and the thieves had taken the two copies. He represented one of them as the original they had given him.

'What do we do now?' he asked.

'We wait,' said Annabel. 'At least we wait until I get the feeling that something is going to happen.'

The feeling came next day. Annabel was in her workshop when she felt that something was strange. She tuned in her crystal ball and to her surprise found it showing a very obviously French sumptuously furnished room containing two well-dressed men talking to a third, obviously the owner of the house. They produced the picture and she could see them carefully unwrapping it. She then saw the horror on the purchaser's face as he inspected the picture.

'It was the painting of a cow's head,' she explained to Henry and Betsy later. 'I got Tommy to paint a cow's head underneath the real picture and after they had wrapped it up for transport I faded out the haystack picture and brought the cow to the surface.'

'Serves them right,' said Henry, 'but won't they be back to see Tommy?'

'Why should they,' said Annabel. 'After all it was the right picture when they left and they obviously hung what they thought was the original back in the house. They will probably think that another thief switched it somewhere on route.'

'I hope you're right,' said Betsy. 'I wouldn't like Tommy to be in any trouble.'

'He won't be. I will see to that, but now we have work to do. The original picture must be taken back. I have checked that the owners of the house are there so if you will go with me I think the real painting should be returned,' said Annabel.

They decided to go that afternoon and set off in Henry's truck with the painting safely held on Betsy's knee.

The approach to Hinchcombe Hall was long and gravelly. The Hall itself was set in well-cultivated gardens. As they drove up to the front door, coming to a scrunchy halt, a tall man dressed in old clothes came out and waved at them.

'Tradesman's entrance round the back,' he called.

'Stay here, Henry,' Annabel ordered. 'Come on Betsy, front door only for us.'

She marched up to the man, Betsy following with the picture.

'Take me to your master,' she said.

'I am Colonel Hardiman,' the man said.

'Sorry,' said Annabel. 'I don't often make that sort of mistake. We have got something for you.'

'In that case come in,' he smiled. 'I expect my clothes fooled you but we have only just got back and I was off to do a spot of gardening. Come in, come in.'

He led the way into the large front hall and there in the pride of place was the Monet.

'We've got this for you,' said Annabel. 'Open it up Betsy.'

Betsy unveiled the picture.

'My word,' said the Colonel. 'Another Monet, I suppose you want me to buy it. Unfortunately I can't even afford the money to insure this one.'

He took a closer look at it, 'By Jove it's the same picture. How did you get this?'

'It's a long story,' said Annabel, 'but sufficient to say that while you were away thieves broke in and stole the painting, substituting a copy. This is the real one.' She indicated the one that Betsy was holding.

'Hold it up by the other one, my dear,' said the Colonel. 'Yes, they really are identical but how do I know you are telling the truth? Perhaps you are just trying to switch a copy for the original.'

Annabel looked affronted but then saw the smile on the Colonel's face.

'Just joking,' he said. 'Let me let you into a secret. This isn't the original, it's a copy. My grandfather had this copy made and sold the original way back in the early 1900's. It was the only way he could keep the Hall going and I know just how he felt about that. This place just eats up money. So you see copy or original copy it doesn't really matter. Will you stay for tea? Dorothy my wife has made some rather scrumptious scones. Do stay.'

Dorothy turned out to be a tall fair-haired woman dressed in blouse and slacks. She welcomed them into the sitting room, sat them down and dispensed tea and scones. Betsy went to fetch Henry who had stayed in the truck.

After introductions had been made Annabel proceeded to tell Dorothy and Arnold Hardiman the whole story.

'I thought someone had been in the house,' said Dorothy. 'When we came back, the kitchen window was slightly open and I thought I had closed it firmly before we left.'

'Don't you have a burglar alarm system?' asked Henry.

'We did,' said Arnold, 'but it broke and I haven't had it fixed.'

'I think you should,' said Henry. 'If you like I can come and fix security bolts to the windows. I can also have a go at mending the alarm system.'

'That's very nice of you,' said Arnold, 'but I'm afraid we are as poor as church mice.'

'Don't worry about that,' said Henry. He looked at Annabel. 'I would be pleased to do it for you.'

'In that case, yes please and accept the picture on the wall as payment.'

He took Tommy's copy down, handed it to Henry and put the original picture back in its place.

In the truck afterwards Annabel said, 'That was a nice offer Henry. It must take a lot to keep a house like that going.'

'Yes, but what are we going to do with the picture?' he asked.

Betsy who was holding it said, 'Give it back to Tommy, it's his by rights.'

And what Tommy did with it nobody knows as there was no wall space in his caravan.

Talent will out

One thing you could say about Happy End is that it is never still. It organises dances, jumble sales, scarecrow competitions and now the latest was a talent competition.

This time the idea hadn't come from the pub but from a most unlikely source, the Pettit sisters. Rosemary had been a singer of romantic ballads in her youth and suddenly felt the urge to get up on a stage again and sing. So she suggested to Alistair Harding, the vicar, that they hold a talent competition.

'There must be lots of talent in the village,' she said.

The vicar was worrying about the church roof and thought that they might use the idea to produce funds for the roof. He put it to Annabel when next they met.

'Why don't you turn it into a talent show,' she suggested. 'In that way it won't be a threat to anyone and the proceeds from the show can be spent repairing the roof.'

So, it was agreed. The vicar offered to act as organiser and the word went out round the village. The response was surprising, everyone seemed to have some talent: juggling, conjuring, singing, reciting monologues. Three sisters, from the new houses whom no-one had really noticed before, came up with the idea of a Moulin Rouge dance routine.

When all the ideas came in, the vicar was overwhelmed. As he said to his wife Victoria at breakfast. 'There's no way we can fit everyone in. We need auditions and a selection committee to pick the acts that will appear in the show.'

To help him make the selection, in addition to himself he picked two other people: Annabel as she had suggested the idea, and Tommy Tucker the artist as he was the nearest thing to art they had.

A date for the auditions was set, and a rehearsal was scheduled for two weeks before the show. Publicity was arranged through the local paper The Barrow Magna Guardian. A one page advertisement was also put through every door, both in Happy End and Barrow Magna, by the newspaper boys.

When Ken Jenkins, reporter for the local paper, heard he came to discus it with Alistair.

'I have a contact in the local TV station, Westerum TV,' he said. 'They might be interested in filming something from the rehearsal to give the show publicity.'

'Every little helps,' said Alistair gratefully. 'I hope you will come to the show and write a report for us afterwards.'

'Of course,' said Ken. 'We can also get a photograph in the paper. I will bring along a photographer.'

*   *   *

The village was in a frenzy of preparation and if we could have looked through the windows of most of the houses and cottages we would have seen costumes being made, lines being learnt, dance routines rehearsed. Audition day came, fortunately a brilliantly sunny day as the queue of potential performers stretched outside the village hall and across the field. Henry, who volunteered to arrange the scenery for the show had the idea of opening up the old scout hut beside the new hall so that people didn't have to queue but could go into the old hut to get ready.

'The only thing that worries me,' said Alistair. 'This show was supposed to promote co-operation between members of the village but they are so competitive you would think that they are bitter enemies.'

Tommy Tucker smiled. 'That's just the artistic talent coming out,' he said. 'Don't worry; it will all sort itself out. Let's have the first one in.'

*   *   *

It is probably best to draw a veil over the auditions. Suffice to say that some acts were good, some were passable, and some were awful. Alistair, being a kind-hearted man couldn't bring himself to tell the awful ones just how bad they were. Annabel saved him by suggesting that after selecting the best for the show the rest were told that there were too many applications and regrettably they couldn't use everyone.

They finally picked Rosemary Pettit to sing romantic songs. They couldn't really leave her out as she had suggested the idea in the first place and in any case her voice, although not strong was pleasant and most of all was on key, which a number of the other potential singers were not. The other singer they picked was Beryl Blackburn who had what Tommy described as a sweet voice and, being younger than Rosemary, had a more modern repertoire. Jack Jennings, the postman, was picked to do monologues such as 'The boy stood on the burning deck'. He delivered these with dramatic gestures, nearly knocking over a chair in his enthusiasm. The Moulin Rouge sisters were picked, together with a juggling act by Richard Brown of the Fox's Revenge.

'If I can juggle the books at the pub,' he said, 'I can juggle anything.'

At first he wanted to juggle with flaming torches but was dissuaded by the vicar who explained that even if it didn't contravene health and safety rules he certainly didn't want the village hall burnt down. Richard promised to practice with less lethal objects.

Olive Garner's husband Bill gave a surprisingly good rendition of the Major General's song from Gilbert and Sullivan's 'Pirates of Penzance' but they had to disappoint Mollie Pike who wanted to show off Spot, her dog.

'He can do tricks,' she said desperately, after getting him up on stage where he refused to perform.

'I'm sorry, Mollie, but we can't risk dog stage fright,' said Annabel.

'Oh well, another time perhaps,' Mollie gathered up Spot and took him back down into the hall.

The youngest performer to audition was Tony Raven, dressed in top hat and tails. Betsy who had come to watch gave him a special clap as he walked onto the stage.

'I need a minute to set up my table,' he explained, 'But of course on the night everything would be ready,'

They waited while he fumbled with the collapsible table and finally he launched into his conjuring act. It wasn't meant to be funny, but like Tommy Cooper's act, everything Tony touched seemed to go wrong. Everyone in the hall apart from Betsy laughed until the tears ran down their cheeks. As Tony got more and more upset things seemed to fall apart. Bunches of flowers came out of his sleeve at the wrong moment, a plastic rabbit shot out of his top hat and his flags of all nations trick tangled up in his tails so that he had to ask someone to come and rescue him.

'We have got to have Tony,' said Tommy Tucker laughing.

Looking very young and blushing red, Tony said, 'It will be all right on the night, I promise.'

Annabel looked at Tony. Yes, I'm sure it will, she thought.

'Now,' said the vicar briskly, 'let's review what we have.'

'I know one thing we don't have,' said Tommy.

'What's that?' asked Annabel.

'A comedian,' he said. 'No-one has come forward to tell jokes.'

'How about you?' suggested Alistair.

'Not me,' he said, 'But I may be able to help. One of my drinking partners in London was Eddy Langford.'

'He's a famous comedian,' said Betsy who was listening to their discussion.

'He is indeed,' said Tommy, 'and I'm sure he would do it if he is free.'

As luck would have it, he was free and Tommy agreed to go to London to meet and brief him on the show.

'He won't come to the rehearsal of course but he neither will he charge a fee if he knows that this is for charity.'

'Make sure he also knows this is a family show,' said Alistair who was a little worried about the sort of jokes a London based comedian might tell.

'No need to worry about that. I've known Eddy a long time. He will do a good job for you.'

'Right, all we have to do now is to time the acts and put them in order. Mr Langford will be the star attraction so we shall put him at the top of the bill.'

Surprisingly, Eddy Langford not only wanted to help but also agreed to come to the rehearsal.

'Just to get the feel of things,' he said.

Accommodation was arranged for him at the Fox's Revenge where Tommy Tucker met him for a drinking session the night before the rehearsal. Eddy soon had the pub in uproar with his jokes.

'If he is as good as that in the show,' said Tommy to Annabel next day, 'he will knock them in the aisles.'

Unfortunately, Westrum TV were unable to come to the rehearsal, but they promised to advertise the show on the local news and would attend the performance in two weeks time.

The rehearsal went as all rehearsals go some good things and some bad. Henry, with help from the younger boys, had devised a backcloth and scenery depicting an old fashioned music hall with potted palms at the sides of the stage. Jack Jennings, of course, swept one of the palms over with his expressive gestures. Henry made a mental note to move it when Jack was on stage. The Moulin Rouge sisters mistimed their dance routine and Richard dropped one of the pint tankards he was juggling. Young Tony's magic act was much better but then it came to Eddy Langford's act. In the pub the night before he had been brilliant, but this time his jokes lacked sparkle. He lurched off the stage after his act and hid in the room he had been allocated as his dressing room.

Alistair Harding was very upset.

'If he performs like that on the night the show will be a complete disaster,' he said.

Unfortunately, Tommy Tucker wasn't there to talk to him so Annabel volunteered to go back stage and have a word.

She went round and knocked gently on his door. Getting no answer, she eased the door open to see Eddy hunched up in a corner looking miserable.

'Go away,' he said. 'I don't want to see anyone.'

Annabel sat down beside him.

'It must be difficult making people laugh all the time.'

He looked up at her. 'You have no idea,' he said.

The story took a little while but eventually it all tumbled out.

As a boy, Eddy had been the smallest in his class at school and had suffered from the bullying of the larger boys. To protect himself he had started making jokes as he found that although he wasn't physically strong he could hit back with words that made others laugh. This determined his career path. Soon he was doing an act in pubs and clubs where a London agent discovered him. His career took off and in addition to a tour of the country, he had his own show on television, appearances at London theatres both as a solo act and as comic characters in plays. But he was not a happy man. Like clowns whose makeup usually includes a wide smile drawn on with greasepaint if you look at their real mouth you often find it set in a hard grimace. It was like that with Tommy. Outside he was the jovial comedian he had always been, whereas inside he was suffering from a lack of confidence and wanting to become free of the persona he had made for himself.

'I just want to be happy,' he told Annabel.

'There's no magic formula,' said Annabel. 'Being happy depends entirely on how you think and feel.'

'At the moment I feel down and out,' he said. 'The reason I could come to your rehearsal is that my bookings are falling off. Sometimes I am a great success and at other times a flop. Well you saw it for yourself this afternoon. People are starting to drop me.'

'You are staying overnight aren't you?' asked Annabel. 'Instead of going straight back to London I want you to come to see me in the morning. Will you do that?'

'Do you think you can help me?' he asked.

Annabel looked at him. 'Of course,' she said. 'Come to the Garden Centre at ten o'clock tomorrow.'

*　　*　　*

At ten o'clock precisely Eddy ambled in to the Garden Centre where he was met by Henry who directed him to Annabel's workroom in the old potting shed.

'Come in, Eddy,' she said setting aside the potion she was working on.

He looked around at the shelves with all sorts of bottles, jars, dried plants, herbs, mixing bowls, instruments, ladles, an egg timer and books of all shapes and sizes. The table was covered with Annabel's latest experiments. Open in front was the large leather-bound spells book in which she recorded her results. She quickly closed it as he came up to the table.

'You're a witch,' he said.

'Don't look so surprised,' Annabel smiled. 'The proper term is wise woman these days but it sometimes involves a bit of magic.'

She put her hand on the leather-bound book. 'Spells handed down over three generations.'

'Do I need a spell?' asked Eddy.

'No, you just need a bit of common sense,' she said.

They discussed his hopes and fears, Annabel suggesting a course of action. The main things she told him were as follows:

* Being happy is a state of mind, not the acquisition of material goods and wealth. Of course, you need enough money to live on but the way you look at the world is important. Also the way you interact with people.

* You won't always feel positive but try to radiate a positive attitude. You don't need always to be telling jokes although you are obviously very good at that. Being nice to people and helping them makes you feel good and helps others.

* This won't work immediately, you need to practice and stick to it for at least a month. By that time, your brain will have reprogrammed itself and things should go well for you.

* Go on stage confidently; reach out to your audience. Smile and they will smile with you. Once you hold them in the palm of your hand, you can't go wrong.

* When you are off stage be nice to people, help them and they will help you. You will notice a tremendous improvement in your life, friends and happiness.

'I feel as though I'm walking on air,' Eddy said shaking Annabel's hand. 'I'm off to London now but I will be back for the show and I hope you will see the improvement in me.'

* * *

The day of the show dawned. Tommy Tucker was worried as there was no sign of Eddy Langford. He went to see Annabel.

'I thought Eddy would come down last night,' he said. 'But there is no sign of him. I rang his phone number in London but he has got his answering machine on.'

Annabel had also been worried but looking in her crystal that morning knew he was on his way.

'Don't worry,' she said. 'He will be here.'

He turned up on the lunchtime train at Kemble and took a taxi to the Fox's Revenge.

'Am I glad to see you,' said Tommy who was lunching in the pub.

'Sorry about that,' said Eddy. 'I had an unexpected engagement at a club in Central London last night. The turn they booked had fallen ill and I took his place. There was no possibility of warning you but I knew I could make it in time today.'

Alistair Harding and Henry were so busy with last minute arrangements that they had hardly noticed the absence of their star comedian.

When he heard, Alistair breathed a sigh of relief. 'I just hope he will be all right tonight,' he said.

The show started at seven o'clock but a dress rehearsal was planned for that afternoon. Eddy Langford excused himself from this.

'On the night I always like to start fresh with the actual performance,' he said.

He contacted Annabel and asked if she would walk with him that afternoon.

'I ought to be at the rehearsal,' she said. 'But, I'm sure they can manage without me. It's not as if I had a job to do.'

They walked up to Barrow Hill.

'And how have things gone?' she asked.

Eddy looked at her and smiled. 'Well,' he said. 'Since our talk I have tried to take your advice and it is working. I had always thought my agent disliked me and that was why I wasn't getting booked. Now, I understand him better. He has an ailing young son and has been worried out of his mind. I think I have helped him by taking the boy to the hospital for him when he couldn't do it. My bookings have gone up again like that unexpected call last night and I am definitely a happier person. I don't hate what I do, I enjoy it and love the audience reaction.'

'Good,' said Annabel.

They were standing on the top of Barrow Hill looking across at the village below.

'Isn't this a stunning view,' she said. 'Of course, you know that fairies live here?'

'After the help you have given me,' he said. 'I believe everything you tell me.'

They wandered across the hill talking until it was time to go back to the village.

'Come in for a spot of tea before the performance,' she said.

'I would be glad to,' he said. 'Just a cup though, I tend not to eat beforehand.'

❋ ❋ ❋

Seven o'clock and the hall was packed. People had come from as far away as Gloucester. Westrum TV had set up two cameras, one at each side of the stage, out of audience view. Ken Jenkins was there to make a report for his paper. Annabel and Henry had centre seats in the front row, along with the vicar and Tommy Tucker.

Excitement ran high. The curtain opened a little jerkily and the show was on.

'Curse that pulley,' said Henry under his breath.

To Annabel's surprise, Eddy Langford came on to the stage.

'I thought he was topping the bill,' she said to Alistair.

'He suggested that he should soften the audience up and introduce the acts,' he whispered back.

He was brilliant. After a word of welcome and a few jokes, which had the audience smiling politely at first and then laughing heartily, he introduced the first act.

'The young, the lovely, Beryl Blackburn.'

Beryl came shyly onto the stage dressed in a very becoming blue dress. The audience went quiet as she sang a melody of popular songs. The applause was terrific. Eddy, acting as compere, held the show together, making it seem a logical progression from act to act. Jack Jennings' monologue went well, Richard Brown juggled safely with a variety of non-breakable objects and Rosemary Pettit, dressed in a crinoline, sang 'Come into the garden Maud' and was flattered when they demanded an encore, which she gave.

Then it was time for the magic act. One of the Moulin Rouge sisters brought on the table. Tony Raven dressed in top hat, and tails carefully laid out a variety of objects on it and bowed to the audience. Annabel could see that he was nervous but had decided that if necessary a little magic wouldn't hurt to make sure that Tony's magic worked. She need not have worried. He had obviously been rehearsing and everything went perfectly. Annabel relaxed.

Then it was Bill Garner, who gave his all in the Major General's song from Gilbert and Sullivan's 'Pirates of Penzance'. This was followed naturally by the Moulin Rouge sisters coming on with 'Three little Maids from School' and then breaking into their dance routine which seemed a little strange going from Gilbert and Sullivan to Offenbach but the audience loved it.

Finally Eddy Langford came back for his act. He had changed from his immaculate compere's outfit to become a red nosed tramp. Clutching a lamp post, provided by Henry, he proceeded to give a wonderful performance as a drunk telling stories and waving a bottle about in emphasis. The audience laughed until they cried. Even the most strait laced of them were laughing. Rosemary Pettit who had come round into the audience after her act had never been seen to laugh but she did this time.

The curtain fell and rose again to reveal the performers. There was wild applause and they took bow after bow. When the curtain finally closed Eddy Langford said, 'Everyone round to the pub. Drinks are on me.'

Down in the body of the hall Ken Jenkins went up to the vicar.

'You will be on the local news tonight,' he said,' and I've got my piece for the paper. A great success, you are to be congratulated.'

The hall emptied, the television people packed up their cameras and there was a strange sense of nothingness.

'All that work,' said Henry, 'and now it has all gone.'

'Not all,' said Alistair holding up the takings. 'The church roof should benefit for many years to come.'

Eddy poked his head through the curtain.

'We are all going round to the pub,' he said. 'I hope you will join us.'

And join him they did.

12

Ghosts at the Grange

It all started when Jessica Oakley woke up one morning to find a dead bird on her bed. Prior to this, there had only been the odd sighting of the ghostly nun crossing the courtyard at dusk. This, however, started a series of unexplained happenings that were much more serious.

Jessica was the widow of Harcourt Oakley remembered as a famous Shakespearian actor. Together, ten years ago, they had moved in to the Grange at Happy End and had turned it from a derelict ruin into a comfortable family home. The Grange had been built on the site of an ancient nunnery and the idea of a ghostly nun appealed to Harcourt Oakley's sense of the dramatic.

At first, he had been disappointed that the ghost was not of the headless horror variety but they became used to the occasional sighting of a hooded figure outside, never inside, the house flitting quietly through the courtyard, under the archway and into the garden.

Harcourt died two years ago on stage where he was appropriately playing Hamlet at the Theatre Royal. Jessica almost wished that his ghost would come back to haunt her, as she missed him terribly, but no such luck. If he was anywhere he would be walking the boards at the Theatre Royal.

Jessica had a younger sister Florence, a fluttering helpless sort of woman, married to an accountant called Eric who spent most of his time away from home meeting his various clients. Florence had two children: Roy aged five and Sophie aged seven.

Jessica was so lonely that she invited Florence and her children to stay with her for the summer holidays.

'There's plenty of room,' she said, as indeed there was. 'The children can have separate rooms and if Eric wants to come down I'll give you both the best bedroom with the four poster bed.'

Florence envied her sister marrying into the acting profession but there was genuine liking and love between them, so she accepted.

'The children are really a handful,' she said. 'You live such a peaceful life in Happy End. Are you sure you want us to disturb that?'

Actually, Florence was pleased to get the invitation as she found it difficult to occupy the children during the holidays. Jessica has such a lovely house and gardens, she thought.

Especially the gardens, where the children could roam and play to their hearts content.

Florence and her children moved in for an extended stay and all worked well until Sophie asked Jessica about the lady who walked through walls in the garden.

Florence thought her daughter was being fanciful but Jessica knew that she had seen the nun.

'I think it may have been a trick of the light, my dear,' she said and with that Sophie appeared to be satisfied. Then, some days later, Jessica woke up to find the dead bird on her bed.

At first she thought it might have flown in through the window and had knocked itself out, but she slept with the window closed and the only way in would be through the door and that was shut. It was a young thrush. Shuddering she picked it up by its wingtip, opened the window and dropped it into the flower bed beneath.

You know how you feel when something unexplained happens: it's as though every hair on your body stands on end. She shook herself and turned her thoughts to the day ahead.

Unfortunately the dead bird was only the first of a number of incidents. At first, they were quite minor. A chair moved to another part of the room, flowers spilled from a vase. Then the poltergeist, if that is what it was, began to intensify its activities.

Sophie and Ray were delighted at the happenings and Sophie reported having seen the nun coming down the stairs as she went to bed the night before.

Jessica became more and more alarmed. She knew that the nun had only been seen in the garden. Something must have disturbed her, probably whatever was causing this series of incidents.

The climax came at dinner that night when the large portrait of Harcourt Oakley, dressed as Hamlet, rose from its hook over the fireplace and crashed down on the stone hearth, shattering the glass into a thousand pieces. Jessica took one look at it, gave a cry of horror, and rushed from the room.

Something had to be done, but what? She thought of exorcism and was about to ring the vicar when Florence dissuaded her.

'I've heard that invoking the Church can sometimes make the situation worse. Isn't there anyone else you can ask? What you want is a professional ghost hunter.'

Jessica had an idea. 'Would a witch do?' she asked.

'They deal with magic and all that sort of thing. Do you know one?'

"Mrs Witchell at the Garden Centre in the village is known to be a witch, but I don't know much about her.'

'Ah,' said Florence. 'You have a wise woman in the village. She should be able to help.'

Annabel was invited to tea at the Grange.

Jessica was old fashioned so they had thin cucumber sandwiches for tea.

'Have one Mrs Witchell, they are delicious.'

Florence, Jessica and Annabel were in the sitting room. The children were out playing in the garden.

Jessica had been nervous at inviting Annabel as she had heard all sorts of stories about her, mainly from the Pettit sisters. She was therefore surprised to find that Annabel was apparently a very ordinary countrywoman with a round face, red cheeks and a cheerful disposition.

'She can't be a witch,' she whispered to Florence as they brought the sandwiches, cake and tea from the kitchen.

'I've told you,' said Florence. 'She's a wisewoman. That's not quite the same thing.'

Jessica found Annabel very easy to talk to. She told her all about the happenings.

'They seem to be getting worse,' she said. 'That picture jumped off its hook in the dining room. We put it in here for safety.' She indicated the frame now reclining again the wall.

As she said this the large vase on the mantelpiece rocked forward and was about to come crashing down.

Annabel saw it out of the corner of her eye and with a quick thought pushed it firmly back on to its base.

'I begin to see your problem,' she said going over to the vase and lifting it up gently.

'I think I know how to stop this. I am going to put a spell on your house so that everything becomes so heavy that it won't move. We'll see how your poltergeist copes with that.'

There was a little scuttling noise at the half open door. Annabel darted to it but there was nothing there.

'Can you really cast spells?' asked Florence.

'Of course,' said Annabel. 'But I don't think it will be necessary now.'

Florence gave her a puzzled look.

'Don't worry, my dear,' she said to Jessica. 'I think I can promise you some results fairly soon.'

'What did you mean, it won't be necessary now?' asked Florence.

'For one thing, if I were to make everything in the house heavy you wouldn't have any dinner as you couldn't lift anything in the kitchen to make a meal. Also, my spell wouldn't have stopped a real poltergeist. I think we shall soon have some results for you but don't be surprised if something does happen tonight. I will be back in the morning.'

Annabel went home and after their evening meal went into her workroom to get out her crystal ball.

'Sorry to give you a lonely evening,' she said to Henry, as she went out. 'I have to keep a watch on the Grange tonight.'

She took her knitting with her and settled down in front of the crystal ball. She tuned in to the Grange and then focussed on the children's bedrooms. She could see Roy tucked up in bed with his light on, reading a book.

Sophie's room was in darkness but Annabel could make out a figure huddled under the covers.

She moved her vision downstairs, first to the dining room and then to the kitchen. As she did so, the door of the kitchen opened and a figure slipped into the room. She followed it as it took down pots and pans from the hooks on the wall, piling them up carefully in a heap on the floor. The figure then went over to the fridge and took out the remains of a piece of beef left over from dinner. Taking out a carving knife from the set of knives on the side, it stuck the knife into the beef and balanced it on the heap of pans.

As Annabel watched, the small figure left the kitchen and made its way back up to the bedrooms. It was no surprise to Annabel when it went into Sophie's room and, throwing back the bedclothes removed the pillows that made it look like a figure in the bed. Sophie herself then climbed into bed pulling the sheet up to her chin.

It's time we taught you a lesson, young lady, thought Annabel. She concentrated on projecting the image of an old lady into Sophie's bedroom.

'Good evening, my dear,' said the old lady sitting on the end of the bed.

Sophie, who was not yet asleep, sat up clutching the bedclothes around her.

'What do you want?' she asked, looking very scared.

'I wanted to warn you about playing with ghostly things,' said the old lady. 'It can get you into a lot of trouble.'

'But who are you?' asked Sophie.

'Who do you think?' said the old lady floating off the bed and up to the ceiling. Then perched upside down she grew a long neck and poked her face close to Sophie.

'All this pretend poltergeist stuff has to stop,' she said.

Sophie drew back as far as she could.

'I only did it for fun,' she said.

'It isn't fun when you scare people.' The old lady floated down to the end of the bed and resumed her normal shape. Annabel was having trouble concentrating but thought she could hold the apparition for a few more minutes.

'There are enough real ghosts about without you pretending to add more. Promise you won't do it again.'

'I promise,' said Sophie.

'That's all right then,' said the 'ghost'. 'Now go back down to the kitchen and clear it all up.'

The apparition vanished and Annabel sat back with a sigh of relief.

A very chastened Sophie crept down to the kitchen. Annabel was able to follow her in her crystal ball.

Next morning she went over to the Grange. Jessica greeted her at the front door.

'We had another happening in the night,' she said.

Annabel looked surprised as they walked into the hall..

Jessica went on, 'Yes, all the pots and pans in the kitchen rearranged themselves but nothing else happened.'

'I think you will find that is the end of it,' said Annabel .

As they walked into the sitting room a freshly picked rose appeared from nowhere and fell at Annabel's feet. She smiled and picked it up, smelling the delicate perfume. There was still a bead of dew on the petals.

Sophie came shyly into the room and hugged Jessica.

'I was just telling your aunt that the poltergeist would stop now and it sent me this beautiful rose as a token.' She gave it back to Sophie.

'Do you mind if I walk in your garden for a while?' she asked.

'Can I come too?' asked Sophie. 'Are you a real witch?'

'Is that all right?' Annabel asked Jessica.

'Of course, but don't be long I know your mother wants you to go with her to Barrow Magna this morning.'

They went into the garden.

'I'm glad you wanted to come with me,' said Annabel. 'I can show you a real ghost.'

'You know it was me pretending then,' said Sophie. 'You are a real witch.'

'Better to call me a wise woman,' said Annabel. 'You see there are good witches and bad witches. A wise woman is always a good witch who tries to help everyone.'

'Yes, I knew it was you and I sent the old lady to see you last night.'

'I was very scared,' said Sophie, 'But I'm not scared now.' She held Annabel's hand.

'What did you mean; you could show me a real ghost?'

Annabel walked over to the stone seat by the ruined wall.

'Sit down here and we'll see,' she said. Sophie perched on the seat beside her.

'You can come out now,' said Annabel. 'I know you don't usually show yourself in the daylight but I want to tell you something.'

Slowly, reluctantly, a kind of mist appeared in front of them resolving itself into the figure of a nun. Under the cowled hood, the face looked young and timid.

'Don't be scared, Sophie. This is the ghost who really haunts this spot.'

She turned to the nun. 'You will be pleased to know that there won't be any more happenings. Sophie has promised.'

The nun nodded and turned away.

'Wait,' said Sophie. But the nun dissolved into mist and was gone.

A freshly picked rose dropped into Sophie's lap.

13

More Trouble than he is Worth

Annabel was visiting Hetty Blackburn who lived in a cottage at the north end of the village. It was Annabel's practice to visit the sick, lonely and elderly of the village taking them some goodies but mostly giving them someone to talk to.

Hetty wasn't elderly but she was certainly lonely although she had her daughter Beryl living with her. She made her living as a dressmaker and had little time to mix with others in the village unless they came to her asking for a dress to be altered, or for something to be remodelled.

Hetty called herself a widow but the truth was that her husband had walked out on her ten years ago.

'Ten years ago,' Hetty reminisced. 'He lost his job up at the farm and that day he just walked out of the door and never came back. I thought he was going down to the shop to get some cigarettes. I even asked him to get some ginger biscuits. I never got them. Been off ginger biscuits ever since.'

'Have another cup of tea, my dear,' she poured more tea into Annabel's cup.

'I miss him sorely,' she said. 'I still don't understand what happened. We was as happy as, well, a couple of tabby cats. Of course, we had the occasional yowl at each other but that weren't nothing. Have a shortbread biscuit.'

Annabel noted that there were no ginger biscuits on the plate. She took a biscuit and gazed obediently at Hetty, nodding slightly in all the right places. In truth, her mind was far away. She was thinking about the batch of remedies that she had brewed that morning.

Did I put the cowbane in the indigestion mixture? She wrinkled her brow but then was brought back to Hetty and her loss.

'I wish he would come back,' Hetty was saying. 'Its such a trial to do everything yourself with no man about the house. Here is a photograph of him. I always thought he was a handsome devil and now he has probably run off with some floozy who isn't worthy of him.'

She laid a photograph in front of Annabel.

'That's me,' she said, 'and that's him,' pointing to the smallish man standing beside Hetty's towering presence.

Annabel felt that she was called upon to say something at this point.

'What would you do if he walked back into your life after

all these years?' she asked.

'First, I'd give him a clip round the ear and ask him where he's been. Then I'd make a fuss of him, sit him down in front of the fire, bring him his slippers and give him some of his favourite cake that I had just baked for him.'

Annabel thought for a moment and then said, 'I can bring him back if you want me to.'

Hetty knew that Annabel was a witch. She weighed the idea up in her mind.

'No, I don't think so,' she said. 'Kind of you to offer but I reckon he'd be more trouble than he's worth.'

'A sensible decision,' said Henry later when Annabel told him about her visit to Hetty. 'Ten years is a long time and people can change a lot over the years.'

'Not you,' said Annabel, looking lovingly at him. 'You are still the same messy old thing you have always been.'

Henry put his arm round her and gave her a hug.

'Come on you two,' said Betsy. 'You're too old for that sort of thing.'

Betsy, their daughter, was just seventeen and had definite ideas about 'the old folk.'

'Never too old, my girl,' said Annabel. 'I'll bet that young Lloyd gives you a hug now and again.'

Betsy blushed and turned her face away pretending to be busy picking up the dishes from the table.

'I could have brought him back for her,' said Annabel. 'Just a bit of pulling magic using that photo. I'd have had him back in a jiffy. That is if he is still alive.'

'Well, she didn't want it, so forget about it,' said Henry giving her another hug.

* * *

Next day Annabel was in her workshop with Betsy helping her to grind up a batch of herbs when in came Bella Blackburn. She was given to dropping in to see Betsy to tell her about what she called 'the goings on' at the Manor.

Annabel had helped Colonel Trevor Blackley get rid of two scheming servants who had attempted to poison him, sending them up to Edinburgh with their memories wiped clean. The Colonel, having learnt his lesson, now used only local labour at the Manor. Bella went in every day and 'did for him' as she put it. He had also approached Mollie Pike to cook for him.

Since the poisoning episode, Trevor Blackley had expanded his horizons, holding dinner parties and inviting a variety of artistic friends. Tommy Tucker was a favourite guest and he was always glad to come to a proper house as a change from his caravan.

Having to clear up after the parties gave Bella an inexhaustible source of stories about the 'goings on' although in truth these were nothing more than the usual happenings at parties.

Bella had been too young to remember her father when he walked out on Hetty and herself but as soon as she could, she vowed to help and support her mother. She had done a variety of things before coming to the Manor, mostly temporary cleaning jobs. Now that she was in more regular employment she felt more secure and she and her mother lived reasonably on her money and the money that Hetty earned from her dressmaking.

✻   ✻   ✻

Things moved on at their usual slow and steady pace in Happy End only to be disturbed one day by the vicar calling on Mrs Blackburn.

'I've received a letter,' he said. 'I would like you to read it.'

Hetty put her glasses on and took the letter written on thin blue airmail paper. It was quite a short letter asking the vicar if Hetty still lived in the village. Signed Albert Blackburn it explained that he had been living in New Zealand but now he was getting older he wanted to return to his roots. He would be returning to this country in three weeks time and wanted to come to Happy End.

She took off her glasses and sat down with a bump.

'The letter is dated three weeks ago. I've only just received it. It must have been held up in the post. I thought you ought to be told as soon as possible.'

Hetty looked absolutely shattered.

'He can't come here,' she said.

'Come now, Mrs Blackburn. If this is Albert then he is your husband.'

When Beryl came home from the Manor, she found her mother in a state of shock.

'I don't rightly know what to do,' she said. 'Ten years is a long time and why did he walk out in the first place?'

This was answered a day or so later when a taxi drew up outside Hetty's cottage and a smartly dressed figure got out and knocked at the door.

Hetty answered the door, took one look at the man standing there and immediately fainted. Albert stepped forward and tried to catch her but Hetty had gained a lot of weight since he had seen her last and all he managed to do was to lower her gently down on to the door mat.

Later, when she revived, she felt ready to face him after she had busied herself in the kitchen making a cup of tea. Albert was sitting in his accustomed place by the fire, in the chair that she had made her own over the years.

'Well, Hetty my love,' he began.

'Don't you Hetty my love me,' she said. 'What you need is a good thrashing. What did you mean by leaving me all those years ago?'

Albert looked sheepish.

'I've brought you some ginger biscuits,' he said. 'Just like you asked.'

Hetty turned over the packet in her hands and spoke in a softer tone.

'Why did you do it Bert?'

He took her hand and said, 'I know now I was wrong but at the time I had just lost my job and felt I had let you down. I wanted to walk out on the whole thing. I went down to Southampton and worked my passage on a boat to New Zealand where I got a job on a farm. I was lucky, I worked my way up to foreman and when the old man died he left me the farm in his will. He had no sons to leave it to and his wife had died years before. So, you see before you a successful man. I sold the farm before I left New Zealand and all I want now is to settle back here with my wife and look after her.'

Hetty had remained very quiet while he told his tale and now she collapsed sobbing on his shoulder. He patted her gently on the back.

When Annabel heard of the return, she immediately went over to see them and was introduced to Albert.

'You are the second visitor today,' said Hetty. 'Them nosy Pettit sisters were here before you. They have only just gone.'

'Trust the Pettit's,' said Annabel as she looked hard at Albert Blackburn. What she saw was not the man she had seen in the photograph but a strapping healthy figure, still small in comparison with Hetty but strong, self-confident and bursting with energy.

'What will you do now?' she asked.

'I've got quite a bit of money,' he said. 'Enough to keep us both comfortably for the rest of our years and now I've met that daughter of ours, well I need to think it out but everything is going to be grand.'

Beryl had been surprised to find that she really had a father.

'But,' she confided in Betsy. 'I can't take to him somehow. There is nothing I can put my finger on but the things he says about his success in New Zealand somehow don't ring true.'

Betsy told Annabel and Henry about this.

'It must have been a shock to both of them,' said Annabel. 'A long-lost husband walking in like that. They will settle down.'

But they didn't.

At first, everything went well. There wasn't much room in the cottage as Hetty had taken over the spare room for a sewing room. There was an attic room up under the eaves and Albert declared that this would do fine as his bedroom.

Gradually a pattern developed. Albert spent most of his time in the Fox's Revenge. He would come back to the cottage drunk until one day Gladys Brown, the pub owner's wife, came to visit.

I don't usually do this,' she said looking embarrassed. 'It's about your husband's bar bill.. Is he in?'

Albert wasn't in and Hetty had no idea where he was. She was working on a wedding dress for a client in Barrow Magna.

'It's like this,' said Gladys. 'Richard wouldn't normally worry about someone local running up a bar bill but your husband isn't exactly local is he? He has assured us that when his money comes from New Zealand he will pay it off. However, it has accumulated quite a bit and we thought we ought to ask for something on account.'

'I had no idea,' said Hetty. 'He has been borrowing money from me saying that he will pay it back soon.'

'Well, if he isn't in, then I suppose we shall have to leave it for now. Tell him I called and that Richard is getting worried.'

'I will,' said Hetty.

When Albert returned he denied all knowledge of a bar bill and when Hetty pressed him, he became angry and abusive.

'He hit Mum,' Beryl told Betsy the next day.

Betsy told Annabel who had also heard of his bad behavior in the Post Office Stores. Apparently, he had gone into the shop for some cigarettes and had been annoyed because Olive Garner was chatting to a customer instead of serving him quickly. He had pushed forward and demanded to be served.

'I think it is time I went to talk to Hetty again,' Annabel said.

She found Hetty in a terrible state.

'That Albert is nothing but trouble,' she said, between sobs. 'He's been borrowing money off me and when I told him he couldn't have any more he hit me.'

She showed Annabel her bruised arm.

'I wish he had never come back. Annabel, can you help me? I know I said I didn't want your help to bring him back but now he is back and he is more trouble than he's worth. What can I do?'

'Leave it to me,' said Annabel. 'I think I know how to deal with your Albert.'

*　*　*

Next day Albert was in the pub. Richard had allowed him a pint but had warned him that this would be the last unless he paid up.

Albert wasn't fundamentally bad but he was a rough diamond and a congenital liar. He hadn't inherited a farm in New Zealand. He had been a farm-hand over there and had come back to England with no money and no prospects. He had come back in the only decent suit he had hoping that his wife would forgive him and support him.

As Albert stood at the bar wondering what to do, a stranger came in.

'Drinks all round,' said the stranger. 'I've struck it lucky and want to share my good fortune with you all.'

The usual regulars were in the pub and they all gathered round scenting a good story.

The stranger was a little man, even smaller than Albert. He had a wizen face and large sticking-out ears. He waved a wad of banknotes as he paid for the drinks.

'And there's plenty more where that came from,' he said.

The story the little man told was an incredible one. He said that all his life he had been trying to turn base metals into gold, the old alchemist's dream. He had tried many different ways of doing this, always involving heating the metals to a high temperature. Time and time again he failed. When he was almost out of money, there had been a knock at the door and a stranger with long pointed ears offered him the secret.

'What did he want in return?' one of the regulars asked.

'Good question,' said the little man. 'That was exactly what I asked myself. However, if there was a catch I couldn't find it. The secret turned out to be not heat, but by bombarding the metal with a complex sequence of high frequency discharges you can realign atoms and molecules and change the original metal into gold. With the proper combination of frequencies, any metal can be transformed into any other. There is a fortune in this if exploited in the right way.'

There was some muttering amongst the regulars and one asked. 'So, why are you telling us this?'

'Because,' said the little man, 'although I can turn any metal into gold I need rather a lot of base metal which I must first buy in order to carry out my plan. I need someone to back me and then, once we have the metal, zinc is best, the backer would be repaid one hundred fold.'

Having heard the story the regulars drifted away. Remarks like, 'sounds like a confidence trick to me,' and 'who would be a sucker and risk his money on that,' drifted through the air.

The little man turned to Albert, who had remained at the bar.

'Would you be interested?' he said.

'I would if I had the money,' said Albert. 'At the moment I am financially embarrassed. My money is all tied up in New Zealand. I can't even pay my bar bill.'

'That's no problem,' said the little man.

He asked Richard. 'Let me know how much this gentleman owes and I will pay it.'

Richard looked both pleased and relieved as money was passed over to settle the bill.

'I don't know how to thank you,' said Albert.

'Don't trouble. I have taken a fancy to you. Why don't you come and look at my equipment?'

Albert felt indebted and so followed him out of the pub and up to the large old van parked outside.

The little man held the rear door of the van open and beckoned Albert to step in. He went into the van expecting to find it full of equipment but the inside of the van was bare. As he turned, the door slammed in his face and he was locked in.

That was the last that mortal eyes ever saw of him.

*　　*　　*

'I don't know how you did it, Annabel,' said Hetty. 'I can't thank you enough. I hope he hasn't been harmed in any way as after all he is my husband even if he was more trouble than he was worth.'

*　　*　　*

Next day there was a knock at Annabel's door. When she answered it the little man was standing there.

'I have done as you asked,' he said. 'He is one of us now. He has no memory of his past life. He is an elf like the rest of us.'

The little man did a triumphant jig. 'We have apprenticed him to a fairy shoemaker who will train him. When he is ready he will spend his days making fairy shoes.'

'At least he won't be bothering his wife and daughter any more.' said Annabel. 'I am much obliged to you. Please thank the Fairy Queen for putting me in touch with you.'

The elf looked at her.

'You know the hardest part,' he said.

'What was that?' asked Annabel.

'The hardest part was changing my ears to human shape. It is going to take me weeks to grow them back to their proper points.'

14

Times Past

Indirectly Ken Jenkins, reporter for the Barrow Magna Guardian, was responsible for putting Happy End on the map although this was the last thing that the locals wanted.

Ken had come to Happy End searching for the origin of the name of the village and had been told various versions. In the end, he decided that Henry Witchell's version of the King under the Hill was probably the right one and he had published it in the paper.

National newspapers are always looking for interesting snippets of information and one had picked up Ken's story and published it. Seeing it, a television producer responsible for a programme called 'Times Past' thought that it might be worthwhile exploring. Times Past was a programme where researchers had three days to excavate a site of interest and report on their findings.

The first indication that Happy End had of this was a visit from Owen Jenkins, the producer of the programme, and his team who virtually took over the Fox's Revenge and proceeded to interview the villagers and trample all over Barrow Hill.

Foxy Sparrow managed to stay out of their way. Those who knew the truth weren't saying anything, but inevitably someone talked, probably someone who had picked up the story from the newspaper and really knew nothing about it.

The upshot was that the television team, having made its initial survey, decided that this would be an excellent place to excavate. The hill was public land so they assumed that no permissions were required but they sent a courtesy letter to the local council who responded positively.

Arrangements progressed relatively slowly so that Foxy had time to talk to the King under the Hill, and Annabel went to see the Fairy Queen.

Foxy discussed it with Annabel afterwards.

'The King is worried that they will find him,' he said.

'Tell him not to worry,' said Annabel. 'I've discussed it with the Fairy Queen and she will get the elves who live under the Hill to help them transport the coffin to a lower level and block the entrances.'

'Will that be enough to stop them finding him?' asked Foxy.

Annabel smiled. 'I shall be doing my bit as well. Don't worry.'

* * *

Word got round that the Times Past team were going to excavate the Hill and people began to descend on Happy End. Most of them walked up the Hill pitching their tents and waiting for the television crew. Some arrived in motor caravans and were disappointed that they couldn't drive up onto the Hill. One, rather more adventurous than the others, drove up the track a short while before getting stuck in deep mud thoughtfully provided by Annabel. After that, no-one else made the attempt but the village was clogged with a variety of motor vehicles and caravans. So much so that when the television crew arrived in their vans, they couldn't get into the village. After some confusion, Sergeant Fossett was called in and together with his constable eventually managed to restore order by lining the traffic up on the side of the road out of the village. The television crew were very experienced, as they parked their vans and set off with tents and equipment to reach the top of the Hill.

The scene on Barrow Hill resembled a summer festival. An area at the top of the Hill had been roped off. Men with picks and shovels, cameras and sound equipment were wandering about seemingly aimlessly. A crowd of people squashed together, surrounded the roped off area only parting when a bulldozer trundled its way towards them.

Annabel had considered stopping it as it bypassed her patch of mud still containing the stranded motor caravan but she let it through thinking she could have more fun with it later.

Everyone in the television crew seemed to live out of tents except Owen Jenkins, the producer, and his two assistants who made themselves comfortable in the Fox's Revenge. Whereas Owen Jenkins kept out of the way of the locals, one of the assistants, a short red haired Scotswoman called Angela, made it a point to drink with them. It didn't take her long to home in on Foxy who wasn't going to be disturbed from his usual perch by the fire for anyone. Angela confided in him that the producer had asked her to mingle with the locals to try to find out more about the village and its origins.

'A sort of spy in the camp,' said Foxy gratefully accepting the pint that she brought him. 'Well I can tell you no good will come of this. There's things that should be left alone and this is one of them.'

'Why do you say that Foxy?' Angela was good at getting on first name terms.

'I would have thought that as the oldest inhabitant of the village you would know something about this King under the Hill.'

Foxy winked. 'That's as maybe,' he said, 'but I'm not the oldest inhabitant. Mick Stanton beats me by a number of years. He is into all these new fangled gadgets. Maybe you should talk to him.'

Angela obtained directions to Mick Stanton's cottage but thought it was too late to call on him that night. As her main job was continuity she couldn't spare the time next day but vowed that she would call on Mick after work.

The main problem was that work carried on until everyone was totally exhausted or the light gave out, such is the nature of making television programmes.

Mick knew nothing about the King and Foxy was just putting Angela off the trail. So when Angela did get a chance to go to Mick's cottage she learnt nothing but was very impressed with Mick's computer setup. They got on very well together as the old and the young sometimes do.

Back at the dig Angela reported to Owen Jenkins that although she had met some fascinating characters they were all clamming up on the subject of the King under the Hill.

'It's possible they don't know anything,' he said, chewing on an unlit cigar. He didn't like cigars but felt that he should maintain a certain image. 'Let's get this show on the road.'

Having done this many times the team went into action with precision. Two areas were marked out for excavation. Grass and topsoil were taken off by the bulldozer and three of the team, Fred, Tom and Dennis prepared to use shovels to dig down cautiously to avoid disturbing anything valuable. Meanwhile, cameras followed every action, focussing on the presenter of the programme who moved from area to area explaining what was happening.

The crowd had increased and were pressing on the roped off area as though they wanted to break through it. Annabel was standing unobtrusively in the crowd.

She decided not to interfere with the bulldozer but thought that everything else should break down or misbehave.

The team took a coffee break but on their return to work found their spades had disappeared. They wandered aimlessly about looking for them. When Owen heard about this he chewed heavily on his cigar murmuring something about the thieving people in the crowd although there was no evidence that anyone had broken through the rope barrier.

'Your spades are here,' someone from the crowd called. 'Over here in these bushes.'

Grumbling Dennis pushed his way through the crowd to the bushes, which were some twenty yards from the dig.

'They are here,' he called. 'Come and give me a hand.'

Tom and Fred went over to join Dennis.

'These aren't our spades,' said Tom holding one up. 'Look it doesn't have a handle.'

Owen Jenkins was rather disturbed and, after a few choice remarks sent Angela and Tom to Barrow Magna in the truck to find more spades.

'I don't care what you pay for them, just get them,' he said.

Meanwhile the camera crew, the presenter and everyone else in the team went back to the tea tent. The crowd murmured amongst itself, but when there was obviously going to be a long delay they dispersed back to their tents, which were dotted all over the hill. Foxy joined Annabel and together they made their way back down to the village.

'That ought to hold them for a bit,' she said. 'Everything under the hill is ready so even if they get as far as an excavation there is nothing to find.'

'Good,' said Foxy. 'I shall be glad when they give up and

go home.'

'Oh, they won't do that yet,' said Annabel. 'I have a few other ideas to help them.'

Hot and tired, Angela and Tom eventually came back with a load of shovels.

'We had to go all the way to Gloucester to get them. We emptied the ironmonger's stock but he let us have them at a reasonable price. I promised a mention for him in the programme credits. Now I need a hot bath,' said Angela.

'Not yet,' said Owen. 'There's plenty of daylight left and we have to get on.'

The crowd seemed to sense that things were happening again and people came out of their tents swarming back to the barrier.

Work resumed. Suddenly Fred waved. 'Over here,' he called.

A cameraman immediately darted over to where he was standing holding a piece of bone. Another followed as Owen ambled over to see what is was.

The first cameraman gave a cry of alarm. 'My screen has gone crazy,' he said. 'Take a look.'

Owen peered into the screen of the camera and started back in alarm. Looking out at him was the skeleton of a dinosaur.

The other cameraman, who had just arrived, reported the same thing.

'Maybe it's trying to tell us something. Keep digging,' said Owen.

Annabel quietly removed the images from the cameras and concentrated on putting a dinosaur skeleton just under the surface of the ground.

'Here it is,' yelled Fred as he uncovered more bones. The others came over to look and to help. An almost complete skeleton of a large dinosaur was uncovered. The crowd watching went wild. In their enthusiasm to see, some of them ducked under the rope barrier followed by the rest, once the psychological barrier of the rope had been broken. The top of the hill became a seething mass of bodies jostling for position, tramping on the bones and shoving cameramen and others in the team out of the way.

With great presence of mind, Owen Jenkins scrambled onto the bonnet of the bulldozer and shouting as loudly as he could yelled, 'What do you think you are doing. Stop!'

He had one of those voices that carry even above the noise of the crowd. There was a momentary lull, then everyone stopped moving. Slowly the people at the back retreated allowing those in the front to back up, some picking up those who had fallen in the rush.

For a while, there was silence broken only by the roar of a helicopter that had just arrived. It hovered above them and settled jerkily onto the hillside away from the crowd. The rotors slowed and the pilot came across to Owen.

'I'm ready for the aerial shots when you are,' he said.

'You will have to hang on for a minute,' said Owen. 'We have had a rather surprising find and I want to transmit it back to the studio as an item for tonight's news.'

Oh no you don't, thought Annabel who was standing in earshot.

The helicopter blades had stopped rotating. The pilot went back to his machine looking slightly disgruntled and the crowd of people wavered in their interest between the excavation and the new spectacle of the helicopter.

Meanwhile Tom, Fred and Dennis had continued to unearth the skeleton, which was filmed by the third cameraman whose camera seemed to be functioning normally.

'Get it down to the transmitting truck, get it edited and send it through,' called Owen. 'I'll phone through and tell them to expect it.'

Since all the trucks were at the bottom of the hill in the village, the cameraman and the presenter had to go down the hill to the trucks. The presenter gave a filmed introduction to what they were doing and what they had found and the editor put it together with the shots of the skeleton. The result was one of those items on the news where the newscaster says 'and now over to our special correspondent at the Times Past dig in Happy End deep in the heart of the Cotswolds.'

The engineer transmitted it to the studio in Gloucester via the transmitter dish erected on one of the trucks. This resulted in a call from the studio to Owen.

'What are you trying to pull, Owen. That item you've just transmitted is nothing but a load of wavy lines.'

Owen went wild. He phoned the engineer in the truck.

'Run that item again in the truck and let me know what's on the tape,' he said.

The engineer reported back that it was just as they had recorded it and he could find no reason why it hadn't transmitted.

Owen chomped his cigar. 'Let me have the tape up here,' he said. 'I'm going to fly it back.'

He walked over to the helicopter pilot and explained what he wanted.

Out of breath, the cameraman arrived with the tape.

'Go with the plane and get it back to the studio as quickly as you can.'

The helicopter took off, circled and disappeared into the distance.

Foxy looked at Annabel. 'That was a good try,' he said. 'But what now.'

Annabel smiled back. 'Don't worry,' she said. 'The tape they are taking is blank.'

Work stopped for the day. People went back to their tents which had now become a sprawling mess across the hillside. Although this was not an official site, someone had dug a latrine trench among the trees on the left. The mass of people gave every indication of staying for the duration of the dig.

'The hillside is a mess,' said Foxy. 'What can we do?'

'Let them wallow in it for tonight,' said Annabel. 'We'll see what we can do in the morning.'

That night Annabel woke to the sound of heavy rain. Henry turned over and said 'What's up.'

'Just rain,' said Annabel. 'Go to sleep.'

She went over to the window and opened it. Torrential rain was bucketing down. She hastily closed the window.

Next morning dawned bright and clear. Hordes of people were coming down from the hill, getting into their vehicles and driving off. Annabel left Betsy and Henry at their breakfast and walked out into the village. People were leaving in droves. The television team were standing dejectedly outside their trucks obviously waiting for Owen Jenkins to tell them what to do.

'What happened,' she asked one of them.

'It was terrible,' he said. 'We were in our tents when there was this tremendous rainstorm and a howling wind. It ripped the tents up and we were soaked to the skin. We are just waiting for the producer to tell us what to do.'

'I would think breakfast in the Fox's Revenge for a start,' said Annabel.

'Good idea. Come on everyone.'

As a body, they all made for the pub.

Foxy Sparrow came up. 'I don't know how you did it,' he said, 'but I think you have solved the problem. They're all washed up and won't go back again.'

Unfortunately, he was wrong. Owen Jenkins was made of sterner stuff. He made the team go back up the hill.

'We must salvage the skeleton even if we abandon the dig,' he said.

When they got there the top of the hill was one enormous mudslide. The tents of the people and the team were gone and there was no sign of the skeleton. Some of them scrabbled amongst the mud but there was nothing to be found. Annabel had removed it before they went back up.

'Okay, this is a washout, literally,' grumbled Owen. 'Let's go. We've got a schedule to meet, so on to the next one.'

When they had gone, Annabel went up the hill to see the damage for herself. She stood there for a moment then, looking across at the grove of trees near the top saw the figure of the Fairy Queen.

'Thank you Annabel. Now we can restore the King to his rightful place,' she said. 'You have saved the day.'

Annabel looked puzzled. 'I thought you caused the storm,' she said.

'Not I,' said the Queen.

Annabel looked up at the sky.

'Thank you,' she said quietly.

Exits and Entrances

Betsy was very excited. University term was about to start and she was getting ready to go to the University of Brookshire. Annabel had been busy making sure that Betsy had all the clothes she needed. Henry had checked again with Mick Stanton about the type of laptop computer that she should have and together they had visited the computer shop in Barrow Magna, where a young man introducing himself as Jerry proved most helpful. They came away with what Jerry described as an ultralight laptop together with a printer that doubled as a photocopier. Henry was a bit dismayed to find that you had to purchase the connecting lead separately and further confused when he found out that to connect to the Internet Betsy would have to pay a monthly subscription to a 'provider'.

'I have to be able to get on to Google,' she said.

'Then, I'm sure everyone will be emailing each other. Why don't you get a computer so that we can keep in touch?'

When Henry told Annabel this, she reminded Betsy that witches don't need computers to communicate.

'If you want us,' she said, 'we shall know and of course you can come home as often as you like.'

'Not on the broomstick,' said Betsy.

'No, I don't think the University would take kindly to a broomstick. Just think yourself here and you will be.'

Preparations continued with Betsy setting up her computer and demonstrating how it worked.

'I can write my essays on it and print them out,' she said. 'There are also all sorts of programs I can use.'

'It all seems very expensive,' said Henry. 'I suppose you must have it to be like everyone else but I think you are going to find that ink costs a lot for the printer.'

Henry had bought the equipment for her together with a year's subscription to enable her to use the computer on the Internet.

* * *

While this had been going on Annabel had been keeping busy with her herbs and potions as they were in autumn, moving towards winter when there was always a steady demand for remedies to deal with coughs and colds.

She was currently making up a chest remedy for Mr Cooke who had been poorly for some time. Although his wife was almost as old as he was, she worried tremendously about him. Annabel was a familiar visitor, bringing her remedies to them.

'It's not that I don't trust Dr Everett,' she told Annabel. 'It's just that I don't trust all these new fangled drugs. Old fashioned remedies like the ones you prepare for us are good enough for me.'

As she spent a good deal of time at their cottage, Annabel had quite long chats with Mr Cooke.

'I'm done for,' he said on one occasion when his chest was particularly bad.

'Not a bit of it,' said Annabel to cheer him up but she could see the hand of death creeping towards him.

This autumn particularly seems a time for partings, she thought. He will not be long for this world. Then there's Betsy, a parting of a different nature but a parting no less. How will Henry and I feel when Betsy flees the nest? I know how I felt when the Fairy King spirited her away but this is different.

She confided her fears to Henry that night.

He gave her a hug and said, 'Don't think of it as a loss. She has to make her own way in the world and there's nothing here in the village for her except perhaps Lloyd.'

Lloyd Raven and Betsy had known each other since childhood and because Henry at the Garden Centre had employed Lloyd, they had seen quite a lot of each other recently.

Betsy took Lloyd for a walk up the Hill.

'It won't be for ever,' she said. 'We can write and I'll be home for the holidays.'

'It won't be the same,' he said and for a moment they paused and looked at each other.

Up until that moment, they had never kissed. They had just been playmates happy in each other's company. Now Lloyd took her in his arms and kissed her. She started back looking at him in surprise.

'I don't think you should have done that,' she said. 'Let's go back now.'

They walked back down the hill slightly apart thinking their own thoughts.

* * *

Autumn, when the leaves turn brown and fall from the trees. Autumn when the warmth of summer turns slowly to the cold of winter. Sometimes not so slowly either. Henry who took pride in what he called his 'Weather Station' reported that temperatures had fallen fifteen degrees overnight.

'Soon be frosts,' he said. 'Worst time of year for my plants.'

Many garden centres simply buy their plants in to sell them again at a profit. Henry prided himself that he grew all the plants he sold. He had a series of polytunnels, made from heavy duty plastic stretched over metal half circles, in which he brought his young plants on and with heating protected them from frost. This tended to be quite expensive in the depths of winter and sometimes he lost plants when there was a particularly cold snap.

Although he had employed Lloyd to help him, he realised that he had also been depending on Betsy who had freely given help when she got home from school. He got to thinking about what he had said to Annabel about it not being a loss.

'You're right, it is going to feel strange without her,' he said. 'It feels as if the world is changing but we must think on the bright side. We still have each other and that's the important thing.'

'I'm worried about Mrs Cooke,' said Annabel. 'They have been together for more years than we have and she is about to lose him. I don't know how she will feel without him to look after.'

Having worked themselves into a thoroughly despondent mood they went to bed.

Henry was up early next morning, as he had to deliver flowers to the church for the Harvest Festival. In fact, everyone was gathering flowers and produce from their gardens to decorate the church and give thanks for this year's harvest.

It was also time for the annual harvest dance and this was a special one for Betsy as she prepared to leave to go to university.

The dance took place as usual in the village hall and this year Lloyd came to fetch her. The previous year he had only been allowed to meet her at the dance and had been waylaid by Lucy Baxter.

This year there would be no trouble with Lucy as Betsy intended to keep a strict eye on Lloyd. They were therefore both surprised to see Lucy at the dance accompanied by a well-dressed, tall, dark haired handsome boy.

They weren't the only ones interested in her escort but it didn't take the Pettit sisters long to find out.

'He's the Todd's eldest boy Tony. Come down specially from Hull University,' Emily whispered to her sister. Emily was acting as cloakroom lady as usual and heard most of the gossip that passed through the cloakroom.

'Lucy has landed herself a good one there,' said Eva Raven who happened to be passing.

Usually, many of the older people in the village stayed at home watching television or reading a book, but this year everyone seemed to have come to the dance.

The band consisted as usual of piano, drums, bass and guitar but surprise, surprise, up there with them was Mick Stanton on an electronic keyboard and Foxy Sparrow with an electric guitar. When Betsy and Lloyd arrived they were just getting into full swing, old favourites, new favourites, the band and our two oldest inhabitants seemed to know them all.

There was one face conspicuously absent. This year Henry and Annabel had promised Betsy that they would be there as it would be her last dance before university. Henry was there but Annabel wasn't.

She was at the Cooke's cottage sitting with Mrs Cooke while they waited for Dr Julian Everett who was in the bedroom with Mr Cooke.

He came downstairs shaking his head. He put his arm round Mrs Cooke's shoulders.

'I've given him something to ease the pain. Call me if you need to. Can I have a word with you outside Mrs Witchell.'

'I doubt he will last the night,' he said to Annabel. 'I'm glad you are here. She needs someone with her.'

'Don't worry,' she said. 'I'll stay. Henry and Betsy are at the dance but they know I'm here.'

Julian smiled. 'I had hoped to go myself but I have another patient to see.'

He popped his head back inside the door to wish Mrs Cooke goodnight and then he was gone.

Annabel went back inside.

'What did he say,' asked Mrs Cooke.

'Nothing good, I'm afraid,' said Annabel. 'Look, why don't you have a bit of a lie down here on the settee. I'll go and sit with him for you.'

'I couldn't rest a moment,' she said, 'but it's very kind of you. I'll just rest my eyes for a bit.'

Annabel saw her tucked up on the settee with a blanket round her then tiptoed upstairs to their bedroom. Mr Cooke appeared to be asleep but then she noticed that he didn't seem to be breathing. She took a small mirror from her bag and held it close to his nose and mouth. As she did so, she noticed a kind of haze forming round his body. There was no sign of him breathing.

She stepped back and sat down as the spectral form of Mr Cooke sat up in bed and looked round in puzzlement.

'What am I doing in bed?' he said.

The ghost of Mr Cooke, for that is what it was, looked at her, got off the bed and stretched his arms.

'Annabel,' he said. 'What is going on? I seem to feel very light almost as though I could float away.'

'I think you have passed over, my dear,' said Annabel.

He looked down at the still figure in the bed. 'Is that me?' he said with a shudder.

Annabel nodded.

'What happens now?' he asked.

'So many questions,' said Annabel. 'You had best be going; you don't want to be late.'

The ghost of Mr Cooke was getting more and more transparent.

'Late for what?' it asked again.

'All will be explained to you, never fear.'

The form evaporated into thin air and Annabel sat back with a sigh. She thought for a moment, then pulled the blanket up over the still figure and went downstairs to where Mrs Cooke was snoring gently.

'I only closed my eyes for a minute,' she said. 'How is he? I must have dreamt because he was down here with me but that couldn't be could it?'

'He was saying goodbye, my dear. He's gone.'

Mrs Cooke looked up at Annabel. 'Well in that case I can now pull down that awful shed he built down the bottom of the garden.'

News of a death takes the living in different ways and Annabel knew that when Mrs Cooke recovered from the shock she would grieve in her own way. Annabel had been at many a passing and prepared to stay all night. She telephoned Dr Everett who promised to come over as soon as he could. She also sent a message to Betsy telling her what had happened. She told her that she would be at the Cooke's cottage until the morning. Next thing she was in the kitchen making a strong cup of tea, which Mrs Cooke accepted gratefully. Annabel knew that the tears would come soon.

*　*　*

Annabel's phone call had caught Dr Everett before he went on his way to his next patient who was about to bring a baby girl into the world. He arrived as the midwife triumphantly held the baby in her arms and presented it to the exhausted mother.

One life at its end, another just begun, he thought to himself and being satisfied that everything was in order made his way back to the Cooke's cottage where Annabel was waiting for him.

*　*　*

Meanwhile, the dance was in full swing. Colonel Blackley was dancing with his newfound love Pat Oakley, Augustus

Jennings-Smythe was dancing with Gladys Brown from the pub. Gladys usually kept the bar at the dance but this evening her husband Richard had come in to relieve her. Even Miss Tatt was there but not dancing until Lloyd, prompted by Betsy, asked her to dance. Lloyd was a bit nervous about this as on one occasion he had declared his love to Miss Tatt while under the influence of a love potion administered by Lucy Baxter. He thought she would be a very awkward dancer but to his surprise, she was light on her feet and danced with him as though they had been partners for years. Betsy was pleased to see the look of sheer pleasure on Miss Tatt's face.

Betsy meanwhile received the telepathic message from her mother and went over to tell Henry.

'I must get over there,' he said.

'Don't fret, Pa. She'll be all right. Just enjoy yourself.'

'I can't, Betsy love. You go on with your Lloyd but I'm going home to wait for your mother. Don't let Lloyd keep you out too late.'

This is how it is with life. Most of the village enjoying themselves at the dance. In a darkened cottage Annabel was consoling Mrs Cooke while the slightly less bewildered spirit of Mr Cooke was finding his way to the great beyond as his body lay still in the upstairs room.

Lloyd took Betsy home. They paused outside the front door.

'It was a lovely evening,' he said. 'I know you go to university in a day or so but I hope this isn't goodbye.'

Betsy clutched at him.

'Of course not. I'll be home in the holidays and we can write during term time.'

'You won't forget me,' he said taking her in his arms. 'Once you get up there with all those other students.'

Henry who had been standing tactfully inside the half opened door thought he ought to cough discretely which he did. Lloyd gave a start, quickly kissed Betsy on the lips and jerked back.

Betsy waved to him as he walked away then turned away towards her father.

'How can you be glad and sad at the same time?' she asked.

'Explain,' said Henry as Betsy settled herself on the arm of the settee.

'I'm sad that Mr Cooke has passed away,' she said. 'Mrs Cooke will be on her own now but I'm glad that I have both of you and I have a good friend in Lloyd. People and relationships are important. I'm also a bit scared about my new life at the university but I expect it will turn out all right.'

Henry thought for a moment.

'Life is full of surprises,' he said. 'Exits and entrances, beginnings and ends, but you are just about to begin a new life. Enjoy it.'

About the Author

Paul Newnton grew up in a small village in the Cotswolds. He has worked in universities across the country and has written and edited many academic books and papers. He now edits a leading academic journal. Having always wanted to return to his rural roots, he is writing a series of tales based on a Cotswold village and its surroundings. The first in the series *The Witch at Happy End* was published in May 2010 and is now available to order online. (www.peterfrancispublishers.co.uk) *More Witchery at Happy End is the second book in the series.*